PUFFIN CLASSICS

Making a Mango Whistle

Making a Mango Whistle

BIBHUTIBHUSHAN BANDOPADHYAY

Translated by Rimli Bhattacharya

PUFFIN BOOKS
An imprint of Penguin Random House

PUFFIN BOOKS

USA | Canada | UK | Ireland | Australia
New Zealand | India | South Africa | China | Singapore

Puffin Books is part of the Penguin Random House group of companies
whose addresses can be found at global.penguinrandomhouse.com

Published by Penguin Random House India Pvt. Ltd
4th Floor, Capital Tower 1, MG Road,
Gurugram 122 002, Haryana, India

First published in Bengali as *Aam Anthir Bhenpu* by Signet Press 1944
This translation first published in Puffin by Penguin Books India 2007

10 9 8 7 6 5 4

ISBN 9780143330226

For sale in the Indian Subcontinent only

Typeset in Minion by Eleven Arts, New Delhi

Printed at Repro India Limited

www.penguin.co.in

This is a legitimate digitally printed version of the book and therefore might not
have certain extra finishing on the cover.

Contents

Introduction

I remember my childhood surrounded by my grandmother and grandfather, aunts and uncles, and many many cousins, some younger and others older than me. We all lived together in a house with courtyards and gardens, rambling staircases and mysterious nooks and corners. A house where adults and children did things together. There was always so much happening—picnics and pujas, singing, poetry reading, not to forget kite-flying. Each day had a touch of something different. Fun things like waiting for Saraswati puja early in the year, for that was when we were allowed to have the first green *ber*. Later in the year came Kali puja (Diwali), and we stuffed dozens of *anaars* with gunpowder and so on. It was so exciting when we set them off at night to see the fountains of light. Then there would be days when the women would make *bori* out of different kinds of dal. First came the big ones, Papa Bori and Mama Bori, and then we children were allowed to try our hand at making baby boris! There was always a way you had to do everything. For instance, you had to bathe before you began making kashundi, the Bengali version of tart mustard sauce. All these little rituals running through the seasons . . . you picked them up simply by living in an extended family. Of course, they were mostly practical kinds of activities, but the colour, the touch and the taste was always special to the season. It was like being surrounded by art.

Our everyday world appears to be shrinking. Families are smaller, even getting together is difficult. Who has the time to tell stories to their children? Stories that fill you with fear and a delicious thrill at the same time. Life moves on at a different pace. Children have hardly any space to play; they are rarely let alone.

Apu and Durga seem to have all the time in the world, and nature is a part of their lives. Their village, the forests, the vast fields are their playground and they are always wandering off, exploring. Apu runs after the hare, not listening to his father's scoldings; brother and sister walk for miles to sight a train; they are scared of the storm but love getting drenched in the rain; Durga steals mangoes . . . Every little incident is precious. Even Indir Thakuran, who has such a hard life; how lovingly she waters her plant every day. The plant lives on even when she is gone. Durga and Indir share a special relationship, while Apu is very much his mother's boy.

I was moved by the passage where Apu is gazing at the kite flying high in the air, watching it become a tiny speck till it disappears, and longing to be like the bird. But the next moment he is rushing off to the comfort of his mother's embrace. Bibhutibhushan is able to bring out this contradictory emotion. We want to belong to our safe, familiar world and at the same time our imagination is fired by the unknown, the land of adventure, of exciting books, of new places and people . . .

Nature seems to be giving and adjusting, responding to the curiosity of a child in *Making a Mango Whistle*. Life goes on, in a kind of cycle. The films in the Apu Trilogy—*Pather Panchali*, *Aparajito*, *Apur Sansar*—break this cycle; they move forward. Apu is not going to be a village priest like his father, and Apu's son is going to be different. While Manikda (Satyajit Ray) reflects on the conflict between tradition and modernity so well in his trilogy, he himself never lost that childlike sense of wonder. I have seen him work with children and he always shared their feeling of discovery. That is why the children in his films are so beautiful.

The other day, when I had gone to a cricket match it suddenly began to rain. 'Let's get wet,' I said to my five-year-old grandson. He looked at me strangely and asked, 'Why?' I realized he has never experienced the thrill of getting wet in the rain, has never had *ola* (hailstones) picked up from the ground. But then, nature is not the same any more. Parents worry about acid rain, pollution, children catching a cold. Children have so little time and space of their own. They are burdened with studies; they learn from books and computers, before they can find out things for themselves.

This translation wonderfully captures the essence of Bibhutibhushan's novel, all its textures and nuances. And the freedom it expresses. It is a comforting, healing book, and I am very happy a new generation of children will have the chance to read it.

December 2006   Sharmila Tagore

1

Old Indir

The day before had been the eleventh day of the lunar fortnight, when widows did not eat any cooked food. Indir Thakuran, who was a distant kinswoman of Harihar, was breaking her fast in the morning with a snack of roasted rice. Next to her on the veranda sat Harihar's six-year-old daughter, silently tracking the movement of each fistful of roasted rice until it disappeared into her aunt's mouth. The girl threw a despairing glance every now and then at the fast emptying bowl. A couple of times she seemed about to speak, but somehow she never could bring herself to do it. Indir Thakuran munched away with her toothless gums till the bell-metal bowl was quite empty; then, she happened to glance at the little girl. 'O dear!' she exclaimed, 'Never 'membered to keep some for you, did I? My, my . . .'

'Never mind, Pishi, *you* have it,' said the little girl,

although the expression in her eyes was most piteous. Indir Thakuran broke off half of one of the big-seeded ripe bananas she had by her side and put it in the girl's hand. Khuki's face lit up as she took the gift from her aunt and began nibbling on it with great concentration.

'What are you doing, sitting tight over there?' her mother called out from the adjoining part of the house. 'Come away here, right now!'

'Let her be, Bou,' said Indir Thakuran to Harihar's young wife. 'She's just sitting beside me, not troubling me in any way. Let her sit.'

'No,' insisted her mother in a firm voice. 'I don't see why she should be hanging around you at mealtimes. I don't care for that sort of behaviour.' To her daughter she said, 'Come away now. Do as I tell you.'

The scared little girl got up and left.

Harihar Ray's small homestead was on the extreme northern edge of the village of Nishchindipur. Harihar was a Brahmin householder of little means. He supported his family on the slender income from some ancestral property he had inherited and the annual gifts he received—from the few disciples he had—for his services as a priest. The exact nature of the kinship between Indir Thakuran and Harihar was not very clear: she was some kind of a sister from his maternal uncle's side. Indir Thakuran was well over seventy with hollowed cheeks, a back bowed with age, her body stooping forward, and her eyesight nothing like it used to be. She would shade her eyes as if seeking protection from the glare of the sun and peer ahead. 'Who's that now?' she would say. 'Is that you, Nabin? No, you're Raju—aren't you?'

It was said that Indir Thakuran had once been married to a renowned kulin Brahmin who came from western India. The nomadic kulin was one of those who made a business out of his many marriages. He had visited his wife in this village once in a blue moon, so Old Indir was left with a rather hazy memory of her husband. After her parents died she lived at her brother's, where she was sure of getting two meals a day. But unfortunately, even her brother died young. A little after that happened, Harihar's father, Ramchand, built a house on a plot of ancestral land and that was when Indir Thakuran first came to live on this land. Harihar had been training himself as a Sanskrit scholar in Benares and other distant places. Only recently had he brought his wife to the ancestral house; it was Old Indir who had managed here alone for years.

The little girl of Harihar's—whom she called Khuki—was the apple of her eye; Old Indir couldn't bear to part with her even for a moment. She too had a daughter once; her name was Bisheshwari. The girl had been married off as a child and had died soon after. She felt as though it was Bisheshwari who had come back as Harihar's little Khuki after a gap of forty years to a childless mother's lap. However, things did not turn out as she had thought they would. Harihar's wife, for all that she was such a sweet-looking young woman, was terribly quarrelsome. And she couldn't stand

3

Indir. She was forever picking up a quarrel with the old woman over the least trifle.

When the wrangling would have gone on for some time, Old Indir would sling a bundle of clothes in her right arm, wedge her brass waterpot between her waist and the crook of her left arm and declare, 'I'm off, Bou! Catch me stepping into this home again . . .' The old woman would spend the rest of the day in the bamboo forest next to their home, upset and unhappy. By late afternoon, Harihar's little daughter would have found her and would be tugging at her sari-end. 'Get up, Pishi! I'll tell Ma, she'll not scold you 'gain. Come with me, Pishi.' In the darkness of the evening the old woman would come back home, holding on to Khuki's hand. Sarbojoya would make a face and observe, 'Here she comes! As if she has any other place to go to, anyway! Doesn't have a brick to call her own, but she's got her pride alright!' This was a scene that had started taking place within a year of their living together. It had happened many a time and would periodically erupt into the daily routine of the household.

Old Indir lived in a thatched room, long fallen to disrepair, which lay to the east of Harihar's land. Inside, a pair of dirty and torn white saris—the plain kind worn by widows—hung from a bamboo stand. The torn places had been knotted up. As the old woman's eyesight dimmed, she was no longer able to thread a needle or do any darning. When the rents in her saris grew too large, she simply tied one end to the other in a knot. A scrappy-looking mat and a couple of tattered rag-quilts lay in one corner. She also had a heap of cloth scraps tied up in a bundle. They had probably been collected and saved over many years with the thought of stitching a rag-quilt out of them some day. When the sun came out after long months of rain, the old woman would carefully take out the scraps one by one and sun them in her courtyard. In a cane basket there was a bundle with the remnants of a few red-bordered saris that had belonged to her daughter Bisheshwari. A brass waterpot, an earthen pot and a couple of earthen bowls made up her remaining possessions.

She kept some roasted rice in the brass pot. If she got hungry at night she would pound some of it in her little mortar and snack on it. As for the earthen bowls, one had a bit of oil, another some salt and yet another held a bit of palm jaggery. Since she was never sure that she would get them if she asked Sarbojoya, the old woman often picked up what she could from the kitchen and saved them for a rainy day. She hid them in the ancient cane basket that had once been her wedding gift.

It was rare for Sarbojoya to come to this part of the house. But her daughter came every evening and sat down on the worn-out rag-quilt that served as a bedding for the old woman by the open veranda; she listened with rapt attention to her Pishima's fairy tales. After she had heard a couple she would prod her aunt, 'Now Pishi, tell me the story of the dacoits.' Over fifty years ago, a family in the village had been attacked by a gang of robbers—it was a story that never failed to thrill the girl. Indir must have told it innumerable times, but barely a few days passed before Khuki wanted to hear it one more time. After the story came the rhymes.

Indir Thakuran had by heart a regular stock of old-fashioned rhymes. She had been much admired as a young woman for this talent: she effortlessly picked up rhymes from all sorts of places and recited them at will to her female companions on the way to the bathing ghat. Now that she had such a patient and attentive audience after so many years, it became a test of her memory as well. Every evening she recited all the rhymes she could recall to this little niece of hers, so as to keep them from getting rusty. How she loved reciting in long drawling tones:

> O Lalita, my champa blossom,
> Listen awhile, won't you?
> A thief's got 'to Radha's room—

After saying this much, she would pause and look smilingly at her niece, waiting for her to complete the rhyme. Khuki would promptly put in: 'You know the fellow, don't you?' She said it most enthusiastically, with extra force on the 'ddon'tyou', bending her head to the beat of the meter. Khuki found these rhyme sessions most entertaining. She loved them with the same passion that she had for every leaf and berry, every ripe fruit, that grew in the village and in the jungle around them.

To trick her niece, the aunt would sometimes say the first couplet of a rhyme she hadn't recited for a fortnight. But it was hard to trick Khuki; she remembered the rest of it perfectly.

Khuki only stirred from the veranda when her mother called her later in the evening for her dinner. These days, her mother found it difficult to move around much with her swelling body. But for her Pishi and her marvellous tales, Khuki would have been quite alone.

2

The mysterious mewing

Khuki had gone off to sleep as usual. For the last two months her aunt had been away. She had left for the house of another relative in a distant village after the latest round of quarrelling with her mother. There was no one to look after Khuki and she felt very lonely. She wept for her Pishima every night, until, tired out, she would sob herself to sleep.

The sound of voices woke her up that night and she saw that Kuroni's Ma, the midwife, was standing by the kitchen, talking to various people from the neighbourhood. Among them was Neda's grandmother. They all looked anxious and preoccupied. The wind was blowing through the bamboo grove making them rustle mysteriously. The moonlight fell in streams on the veranda and the cool breeze soon put her back to sleep.

She was woken up in the middle of the night by muffled sounds of people running around and indistinct cries. She sat up for a while, but it was all very confusing, so she fell asleep once more. At some point in the night she was roused from her sleep by the sound of a kitten mewing. She remembered with a start Meni Pussy's litter of newborn kittens—she had safely stowed them away only that afternoon inside a crumbling earthen stove. Such soft little bundles they were, their eyes still tightly shut! Oh no! That wretched tomcat must have come to gobble them up, she thought. Only half awake, she hurriedly found her way to her aunt's veranda and put in her hand to the depths of the old stove to check on the kittens. But, no— the kittens were all curled up safe and sound, fast asleep. And there was no trace of the tom either! Puzzled, she returned to her bed and fell asleep once again. But the faint mewing came back again and went on fitfully through her sleep.

The next morning she was rubbing her eyes awake when Kuroni's Ma, the midwife, said to her, 'Khuki! You've had a little brother last night—don't you want to see him? What a to-do there was to be sure all night . . . Where were you all that time?' Khuki made a run for the birthing shed which had been built a little distance away from the house and quickly peeped in through the door. Her mother lay fast asleep, her back to the walls woven of date-palm leaves . . . and next to her . . . a tiny creature—the size of a big china doll—lay sleeping all bundled up in layers of thin rag-quilts. She saw them both dimly through the slight haze that came from the charcoal fire.

As she stood there watching, the little creature suddenly opened its incredibly tiny eyes and blinked away. It waved two thin arms in an aimless manner and then gave out a weak little cry. Only now Khuki recognized the sound she had mistaken for mewing last night. From a distance it *would* seem exactly like a kitten mewing! She was suddenly filled with infinite tenderness and love for this helpless little thing—her brother! But much as she wanted to, Khuki was prevented from entering the birthing shed by Kuroni's Ma and Neda's grandma.

Once her mother was allowed to come out of the birthing shed and begin her household chores, Khuki loved to push back and forth the little cloth-swing in which her brother lay and recite to him all the rhymes she knew. But while she did so, she remembered all those wonderful evenings when she and her aunt had recited them together and she couldn't help crying. What a lot of rhymes her aunt knew!

The neighbours came trooping in to see the newborn boy. 'What a darling Khoka!' they all exclaimed. 'Such a lovely mop of silken hair . . . How fair he is!' As they were leaving they would say to each other, 'And did you see the way he smiles!'

So many people came every day to see Khoka . . . if only her aunt would come and have a glimpse of the baby! Why did her aunt have to leave her and go off somewhere far away? Would she never come back? Khuki was a child herself, but she understood that neither her Baba nor her Ma really loved old Pishima and that no one would bother about getting her back. During the day, if her eyes fell on Pishima's thatched room her heart ached. On some days, the door swung idly, unlatched. It looked so forlorn. The veranda was filled with bat droppings. No one swept the courtyard now; mossy patches, weeds and saplings of sheora and kochu had sprouted up here and there. Her Pishima would've never let that happen! Khuki's large eyes welled up with tears . . . how could she forget all those funny rhymes, those wonderful tales?

Then one day, Hari Palit's daughter dropped in to tell her mother, 'On my way to the ghat, I saw your old woman coming past the pond along the path by the field, with her brass waterpot and bundle. She's stopped at the Chakravarti home and is sitting there right now. Send Dugga to fetch her. Tell her to take her by the hand and bring her back home—that's the only way she'll get over her temper.'

Old Indir was being regaled with stories about her newborn nephew by the neighbourhood girls as she sat waiting in Hari Palit's courtyard.

'Pishima!'

The old woman was startled to see Durga, who was panting away as though she had run for miles to come to her aunt. She leaned forward to hold her little niece and Durga leapt into her open arms at the same moment. The little girl was all smiles but her eyes were wet with tears.

When they had come home the old woman was so thrilled with the new baby that she laughed and cried all in the same breath. He was like a radiant moon shining over their ancestral land after many years.

The next morning the old woman briskly got down to sweeping the courtyard. She plucked out all the weeds and saplings that had sprung up these past few months. The funny emptiness that Durga had been feeling all this time now left her. It seemed like all was well with the world.

3

Khoka's antics

Khoka was now all of ten months old. He was thin and his face, exquisitely tiny. He had only two teeth, both sprung up from his lower gums. At any time of the day, for no rhyme or reason, you would find him proudly flashing those two teeth. People said to his mother, 'Now that's a smile in a million!' You just had to start him off a bit and Khoka would laugh and gurgle without stopping. 'There there Khoka, that's quite enough now,' his mother would say. 'You've laughed a whole lot today—a lot! Won't you keep something for tomorrow, my darling?'

Khoka had learnt two words. When he was happy he showed off his milk teeth and said, 'Je - je - je - je!' And if he was sad or angry he went, 'Na - na - na - na!' and then set up howling in the most awful way. He tried out his teeth on whatever he could lay his hands on—a lump of mud, a bit of wood, his mother's sari—everything was fair game. Sometimes, while his mother was feeding him milk with a shell-shaped spoon, he bit hard into the shiny bell-metal spoon with great delight. 'O Khoka!' said his mother, laughing at his antics, 'Why've you gone and bitten into the spoon now? Let go, my precious. You've only got those two little teeth—however will you smile if you break them, huh?' But Khoka does not let go, not until his mother has put in her finger into his mouth and after quite a struggle eased out the spoon from his fierce hold.

Khuki was too much of a child herself to be constantly minding her brother, so their mother had to make him a special pen out of bamboo. It was placed in the kitchen veranda and she kept an eye on him as she worked. Though hemmed in by the slats like a prisoner in a courtroom, the little fellow laughed away, exclaiming and muttering in his own language to an invisible audience. Sometimes he managed to hold on to the top of the pen and gaze over it into the bamboo copse just outside their home. When he had learnt to recognize the sound of his mother coming back from the bathing ghat, he would immediately look up from his game and wobble into a standing position to welcome her with one of his dazzling smiles. 'Oh no!' his mother would say, 'I'd only just put the kajal around your eyes and you've gone and smudged it all over—you look like a perfect tree pie! Come to your Ma, darling, she'll clean you up again!' When she tried to rub off the kajal, much against his will, his face turned a bright red. 'Na - na - na - na!' he protested angrily. But his mother didn't listen. Since that time, as soon as Khoka saw the towel in her hand, he tried to crawl away from it as fast as he could.

When Sarbojoya would return from the ghat, she said, 'Come, Khoka, can you say too-o-o-o-o? Say too-o-o-o-o! Now, can you go rocky-rocky?' And Khoka would promptly sit down and sway forward and backward, forward and backward. He even had a song to go with his wild swaying:

je - e - e - je - je - je - e - e - e
je - je - je - je - e

From morning to late at night, the lonely house by the bamboo forest rang with the laughter and meaningless babble of the ten-month-old child.

On some days Harihar might be caught up with his accounts or be deep in writing, when Sarbojoya would bring Khoka and tell her husband, 'Why don't you look after the boy a bit? The girl's gone out somewhere and her aunt's gone to the ghat. Here, hold him! How will I ever get to bathe or do anything if I have to lug him around all the time! Keep an eye on him, will you?'

'Uh-oh!' said Harihar. 'Don't bother me with that sort of a thing—I'm really very busy now.'

Sarbojoya would angrily put down Khoka next to his father and go off. When Harihar happened to look up from his work, he would find Khoka happily sucking on one of his slippers. Hurriedly snatching it away, Harihar would exclaim, 'Ooh! What a mess she has got me into! Here I was, working away . . .'

Suddenly a sparrow alighted on the edge of the veranda. Khoka stared in amazement at his father and pointing at the little bird, said: 'Je - je - je - je - e!'

Harihar smiled at him tenderly, all his irritation gone.

4

The end of an era

'Well, Bou! I've come for the two paise that you be owing me!' said Dasi Thakuran with a smile. Dasi lived some distance away, in another part of the same village. 'Aunt Indir bought a nona fruit off me yesterday. Said I was to come and get the money for it today . . .'

Sarbojoya, who was busy with her household chores, stopped in astonishment. '*Bought* a nona off you, did you say?'

Dasi Thakuran's mild manner disappeared instantly. She was a hard-headed businesswoman and wouldn't part with a strand of tamarind or a pair of hog plums or even a bundle of spinach without making some money out of it. 'Ask your sister-in-law then, as to whether she bought it off me or not!' she said challengingly. 'Would I've come lying, first thing in the morning, all for the sake of two paise! Wouldn't have given it for less than four paise—I'm an old woman wanting a bit of fruit, said she—so I let her have it for two!'

Sarbojoya was speechless with rage. A fruit as common as a nona—not even as good as a custard apple—that grew in such abundance all over the jungle around the village, so plentiful that even the cows wouldn't want to lick it . . . She could not comprehend how there could be someone in the village who would actually spend good money *buying* a nona!

Just at this moment, Old Indir happened to return home. Sarbojoya practically fell on her, 'You've had your run of years and are at the end of your life—shouldn't you spare a thought as to *whose* money you're spending so freely? Eating off somebody for all these years: haven't you *any* feelings for his money, squandering it the way you are? You've gone and bought a nona! How am I to feed you if it goes on like this! It's a nona today and something else tomorrow!'

The old woman looked stricken, but she tried to manage a smile, 'Yes, Bou . . . the nona . . . thought I'd eat one, you know . . . it's not too long that I'll live, isn't that so? Give her the two paise, won't you?'

'You seem to think that paise are to be had for the asking,' screeched back Sarbojoya, her voice rising to the highest pitch. 'Got your own pots and pans—sell them and pay her off!' She picked up the pitcher and stalked off towards the ghat without another word.

Dasi Thakuran stood there waiting for a bit and then declared, 'I swear I've never been so harassed for goods that I've sold! And as for you Aunt Indir, if you didn't have a paisa of your own, why buy the nona in the first place? I'm telling you, never you buy things on credit again! Well, the two of you can fight it out. I'm a poor woman, that's what I am. I'll come 'round this evening and you better toss me my two paise . . .'

Khuki followed Dasi out through the outer door of the courtyard, trying to talk her out of her temper. 'Pishima's an old woman, and all she did was to buy a nona: must you scold her? Don't we feel like eating something, Aunt Dasi! And it was such a nice one too, that nona—she gave me half of it yesterday! Do you have a tree in your house, Auntie?' Then she called out again, 'Listen, Aunt Dasi, I'll give you one paisa. I have it inside my doll's box, but Ma locked up the house before she went to the ghat. Let her come back and I'll give it to you secretly, but don't you tell Ma.'

A little before the midday meal Old Indir was seen leaving the house, a grimy bundle hanging from her right hand, the brass waterpot clutched in her left, the old mat tucked under her arm. The border of the mat was torn and the broken sticks were hanging out at odd angles.

'O Pishi, don't go, please,' cried out Khuki. 'Where are you going, O Pishi?' She came out running after her aunt and held on to one end of the mat, 'I'll cry if you go Pishi, I will really!'

Sarbojoya, who had come back from the ghat and was now in their veranda, said, 'Well, go if you wish to; but what's the point of bringing bad luck on *us* by going off at this time of the day without a morsel in your mouth! You ought to have some consideration for the householder whose food you've been eating all these years—and these little children in the family! Do you think it bodes well for us! But you *want* something bad to happen to us, don't you? Isn't that what you want? That's the sort of mean person you are— no wonder you're in this wretched state!'

The old woman didn't turn back. She went to Nabin Ghoshal who lived in another part of the village. Nabin's wife listened to the whole story most sympathetically and exclaimed with her hand on her cheek for emphasis, 'Never heard the like, I'm sure. Stay with us, old woman, you stay here!' After a couple of months at Nabin Ghoshal's, Indir moved into Teenkori Ghoshal's, and from there she went on to Purna Chakravarti. In every house, after the warmth of the initial welcome had cooled down, the inmates would express their displeasure in a number of ways. They would counsel her to go back to Harihar's and sort out differences. The old woman wandered through a couple of more households in this fashion, hoping all the while that at least Harihar would send for her sooner than later. But three months went by and no one came to call her home. This time, Durga hadn't come either. The old woman knew of course that it was quite a distance between the two neighbourhoods and that it would be hard for a little girl to walk all that way. A couple of times she herself walked over to the neighbourhood of her former home in the hope of running into Khuki, but that did not happen.

No one can be a guest for very long. After another month had gone by, the villagers decided that milkwoman Chinta's abandoned thatched hut should be given to Old Indir as a refuge, and that they would all contribute something for her daily needs. It was a tiny room with walls made of wattle, and quite far away from the other houses; in fact, it was right inside a bamboo forest. Word came to Indir from various sources that Sarbojoya had declared to all and sundry, 'Let the old woman test her might! As for me, I'm not going to let her put her head in through this door. No, she's certainly not coming back to *this* house! She never looked back at my darlings and left in a huff wishing us ill. Let her go rot with the dead cattle!'

Those who had promised to help Indir were very enthusiastic to begin with, but gradually they lost interest and became indifferent. 'Why did I come away in such a rage?' the old woman berated herself. 'Bou asked me not to, and Khuki wept so hard and pulled at my hand . . .' The tears flowed down her sunken cheeks as she upbraided herself, thinking of former times. 'Such sorrow I was fated to endure . . . at the end of my life! If only I had the little girl with me . . .'

It was the day of the spring equinox. The sun had been fierce all day though a mild breeze had sprung up in the evening. You could hear the drumbeats from the Charak festival go rat-a-tat in the neighbouring Gosain-para. The Charak fair was still on.

Old Indir, who had been wandering around in the sun from one house to another and had been fretting and brooding for her lost home, was feeling frail and feverish. The fever would come on every evening. She was lying down quietly on her thin mat on the veranda. She had placed an earthen bowl of water by her head. The brass waterpot had been pawned for four annas to buy herself some rice. The fever made her very thirsty: every now and then she sipped some water from the earthen pot.

'Pishima!'

The old woman threw away her rag-quilt and jumped up in her joy. It was Khuki climbing up the steps to the veranda. Behind her came Raji, Behari Chakravarti's daughter, also from the same village as theirs. Khuki had on a fresh sari, the end of which was knotted up in a number of little bundles. The old woman was not able to say much. She lovingly stretched out her thin arms to her niece and hugged the girl to her fevered breasts.

'Pishi, you're not to tell anyone. No one must know I've come to see you secretly on my way back from the Charak fair—and Raji came along with me as well. Look at what I've got for you from the Charak fair!' said Khuki, untying her little bundles. 'Candied rice! I've got two paise worth of candied rice for you and a couple of sugar balls. And I've got a wooden doll for Khoka.'

The old woman now sat up properly. She looked and examined all the gifts carefully, touching them and exclaiming over them. 'O my precious! Let's see them now! Look at how many things she's got me. May you be a queen—such kindness to your poor aunt! Ah! Let's have a look at the wooden doll . . . What a lovely doll! How much did they take for it?'

After a flood of words, Khuki said, 'But Pishi, you're so hot!'

'I've been out in the sun the whole day—that's how I've run up a fever . . . so I was lying down for a bit . . . I thought . . .'

Young as she was, Durga immediately knew why her aunt had been out all day in the sun. She lovingly stroked the thin body, wasted by hunger and sorrow, 'You must come home now. I don't get to hear any stories or anything in the evenings. You *will* come home, won't you?'

The old woman started in pleasure and asked eagerly, 'Oh, was it Bou who told you something today?'

'No, Pishima! Auntie has not said anything at all,' chipped in Raji. 'Auntie doesn't let Dugga come here. And she scolds *us* if we try and say anything. But you must come back, Pishima! If you were to talk to Auntie and tell her everything nicely, I'm sure she wouldn't say anything.'

'You will come tomorrow, Pishi? Ma won't say a thing,' said Khuki. 'I'll be going home now, Pishi. But don't tell anyone that I came, and be sure to come in the morning—'

When she got up the next morning, Indir Thakuran felt a little lighter. She made a bundle of her pair of torn saris and a little later into the day she started her trek home. She ran into Gopi Vaishnav's wife on the way. 'Ah, Auntie, you're going home, I see. Has sister-in-law cooled down a bit, then?' Gopi's wife asked her.

The old woman gave her a broad smile and said by way of explanation, 'Dugga came to call me last evening, you see. "Ma's been asking for you to come back home," she said. How she cried and wept, the poor thing. So I said, "Alright you go home now; I'll set off in the morning and reach home by afternoon." Cried so hard, that girl. Didn't want to leave me at all—so I'm heading back home.'

When she finally reached Harihar's, she found that no one was home. The fever had not left her through the night and after walking all the way in the sun, she was feeling utterly exhausted and even dizzy. She put down her bundle and sat herself down on the stoop.

In a little while, Sarbojoya pushed open the backdoor to the courtyard and came in after bathing in the river. Her eyes fell on her sister-in-law sitting on the veranda steps and she was too dumbfounded to say anything at first.

'O Bou!' said the old woman with a little laugh. 'Is all well with you? Here, now, I've come back after all this while . . . at my age, you know, how am I to live without all of you?'

Sarbojoya walked up to her and said, 'You've come back here—and why, may I know?' Indir's smile faded away at the grim manner in which these words were spoken.

Without waiting for an answer, Sarbojoya went on, 'There's never going to be a place for you in this house, ever. Didn't I tell you so that very day? Then what makes you come back!'

The old woman had grown rigid like a block of wood. Not a word escaped her lips for some moments. Then she burst into tears. 'O Bou!' she pleaded, 'don't speak in that way. Give me a mite of space to rest my bones in. Where can I go to at this age, at the end of my life? At least this bit of land—'

'That's enough now! You don't have to bring in "this bit of land"—much you care for those who live on it. Sleepless nights you must've given yourself worrying about them! Now go—take yourself away, right now! Otherwise, I'll do something terrible.'

Indir Thakuran had probably not imagined that things had come to this pass. Just as a drowning man clutches on to whatever he might find near him, so did Old Indir look around her wildly, seeking to find some strand that she could hold on to. She felt instinctively that today her refuge of many decades was truly slipping away from her and there was nothing, nothing that she could do to stop it.

'Now, go on,' went on Sarbojoya relentlessly. 'There's no

use your sitting here. It's getting on to be afternoon and I've got work on my hands. Can't give you any place here—by any means.'

The old woman laboriously got up with her bundle. Dazed as she was, on her way out she noticed the broom with which she used to sweep the courtyard leaning against the ancient wall. Clearly, no one had touched the broom for the past few months. The green grass around her room, the lemon tree she had planted with such care, the broom that was so familiar and dear to her, Khuki and Khoka, this bit of land that had once belonged to Uncle Braja—this was all she had known for most of her seventy-five years. She was bidding them goodbye, forever.

The Ray family's matron saw her walking away with her bundle tucked under her arm and called out to her, 'Grandma, where are you going back? Aren't you going to go home?' When she got no reply from the old woman, she remarked, 'Gran'ma's gone stone deaf!'

Late that afternoon, someone came running from the Palit neighbourhood. 'O Bou,' she said to Sarbojoya, 'your old woman's a-dying! Been lying next to the Palits' granary since noon. She was walking back somewhere in the sun and just couldn't go on any more. Do go and have a look. Is the Master not home? Do send him there as soon as he comes.'

It was true that Old Indir lay dying next to the Palits' paddy stacks. On her way back from Harihar's house she had felt very ill and after a while had simply collapsed at the Palits'. They had first carried her to the shrine of the Goddess Chandi. They tried to revive her by massaging her chest and feet with warm oil, fanning her, sprinkling water on her. But after having tried out everything they brought her down, for they realized that if anything she was worsening. A number of people from the neighbourhood now crowded around her, commenting and advising. 'Well, why come out in the sun at all! Look how fierce the sun is today!' said one. 'She'll get better soon,' said another. 'It's just a spell of dizziness or something.'

'It's not dizziness,' said Bishu Palit. 'The old woman is not going to live . . . and with Uncle Hari not at home . . . We've sent word. But then, who will come all this distance?'

Dinu Chakravarti's eldest son, Foni, who had come to hear about the old woman's condition, now approached the crowd.

'Thank goodness you've come, Master! Give her some sacred water from the Ganga. A pretty business, this—her not getting to die in a Brahmin locality. We were so anxious about who could give her the Ganga water.'

Foni put his walking stick of bainchi wood in Bishu Palit's hand and settled himself next to the dying old woman. He brought a little scoop of the Ganga water towards her and called out, 'O Pishima!'

The old woman merely stared at him in a dim and confused way. There was no sound from her lips. 'How are you, Pishima?' Foni tried again. 'Are you not feeling well?'

He tried pouring some of the Ganga water into her mouth but it did not go in.

'Try one more time,' said Bishu Palit to Foni. But it was of no avail.

A little later, when Foni gently closed the eyelids of the old woman, a thin trickle of water flowed from her sockets down her withered and ancient cheeks.

The death of Old Indir marked the end of an era in the village of Nishchindipur.

5

The old indigo bungalow

About five years have gone by since Indir Thakuran's death.

It was still cold towards early February. On a late afternoon on Saraswati puja day, a group of people from Nishchindipur were on their way to a field beyond their village, hoping to sight the blue-throated bird. As they walked along the narrow track hemmed in by trees, bushes and scrub on either side, one of the party said, 'So, Hari, have you let out your banana orchard again to milkman Bhushno?'

Harihar was about to say something like a 'yes' when he looked back and exclaimed, 'Where's that boy gone? Khoka . . . Khoka-a-a . . .'

From behind the bend in the path a slender and beautiful six year old came running to catch up with the men.

'Hasn't taken you long to fall behind once more, has it? Come on now, run on ahead,' said Harihar to his son.

'What was that went into the jungle, Baba?' asked the boy. 'With such big ears?'

Without paying any attention to the question, Harihar turned to his companion Nabin Palit to discuss the finer points of fishing.

'What *was* that ran into the forest? With such big ears?' the boy asked again excitedly.

'I just can't keep up with all your questions any more, child!' said Harihar. 'It's only been what's this, what's that, from the time we set off! Did I see what ran into the forest? Now march on.'

The little boy went on ahead as his father had asked him to.

Suddenly, pointing his finger at a clump of thatch-grass reeds, he ran shrieking towards it. 'Here it goes, Baba, it went in here! Look, Baba, big ears . . . here!

His father called out, 'Ohh! Watch out for the sharp edges! You'll hurt yourself.' He came up hurriedly and grabbed his son's hand. 'What a pest you've been! . . . A hundred times I've told you and you won't listen. That's why I wasn't bringing you along in the first place.'

The boy looked up at his father, his face shining with eager excitement, 'What was it, Baba?'

'Did I see it? Must've been a pig or something. Come on now, walk on—right in the middle of the path.'

'It wasn't a pig, Baba: it was this small,' declared the boy as he bent down to show his father exactly how high the creature had been from the ground.

'All right, I've got it. No need to show me. Come on now.'

'That was a hare, little fellow—a hare. That's because there are hares living here in these clumps of grass,' said Nabin Palit.

The boy had seen the picture of a hare in his alphabet book—H for hare. But he had never imagined that one would actually leap in and out of the jungle in real life and that he would get to see it. A hare! And a live one too! One that leapt up and darted away right in front of you. Not a picture, not a china toy—but a real live hare with long ears standing straight! And right here, in these very bushes of bhat and bainchi that sprawled all over the wasteland! Could such a thing happen in the very world in which *he* lived?

Meanwhile, the group had now left behind the narrow path through the jungle and had come upon the open field. As they strolled around, Nabin Palit began recounting how he had made a lot of money by planting a crop of yam beans in the northern part of this same field. Gradually, they got around to talking about how costly everything had become these days, how Kundu's warehouse had burnt down in the Ashadu bazaar, when Dinu Ganguly's daughter was to be married, and such like important events.

'Where's the blue-throated bird, Baba?' called out Harihar's son.

'Right here. Keep a watch, it will fly to that babul tree in a while.'

The boy raised his face to stare at all the babul trees around them. There were also some low trees of common jujubes thick with ripening berries, and the boy gazed at them with astonishment and longing. A couple of times he tried to pick the berries but was stopped by his father's scolding.

'You've been going on about the kuthi . . . Here, Khoka, look! That's the saheb's bungalow.'

An ancient bungalow lay sprawling on the riverbank like the skeleton of a huge and ferocious prehistoric monster. It was a leftover from the old days when the English sahebs had cultivated indigo in huge tracts of the countryside.

The boy was drinking in everything around him. In all his six years this was the first time he had come so far away from home! All he had known of the world so far was his own home and Neda's home and, at the very most, Ranu didi's house. Whenever he would go bathing at the ghat with his mother, it was only the ruined boiler room of the indigo bungalow that he could see from a distance.

'Is that the bungalow, Ma?' he would ask his mother, pointing to the dim shape. He had heard of it from his father, his elder sister and from various people in the village, but now he was actually there! And beyond this field, on the other side—was that the fairy tale land of his mother's stories? The land of Shyam-Lanka where you will find the tree of the fabulous birds—the Bengama and Bengami, under which the lonely banished prince lays himself to sleep, naked sword by his side? On that other side no people lived.

It was the very end of the world, the realm of the unknown and the magical.

On their way back the boy stretched out his hand to pick a bunch of brightly coloured fruits that hung from a vine.

'Hey! What are you doing! Don't touch it—it's cowhage . . . with stinging hairs. You've been such a bother! This is it—I'm not going to take you anywhere, ever. You'll have itching hands and blisters if you touch those pods. Haven't I been telling you to keep to the middle of the path, but you just won't listen!'

'Why will my hands itch, Baba?'

'Because it's poisonous, poi-son-ous. No one ever touches cowhage, little one. All those fine hairs—they would've stung you and burnt you terribly and you would have been screaming by now.'

When they reached the village Harihar picked up his little son and entered their home through the backdoor of the courtyard. Sarbojoya came out to meet them as she heard the backdoor being opened. 'How late it is—and you hadn't taken the cotton shawl to keep him warm.'

'What a bother he has been!' said Harihar to his wife. 'Running off here and there . . . it was hard to keep him by my side. And he was about to grab cowhage pods!'

He turned to his son and said, 'Well, you've been pestering me to see the field by the old indigo bungalow: are you happy now that you've been there and seen it for yourself?'

6

Pickling mangoes

It was eight or nine in the morning. Harihar's son was busy playing by himself in the open veranda of their house when Durga called out suddenly from behind the jackfruit tree in their courtyard, 'Apu, Apu-u-u-u . . .' She had just made an appearance after having been away from home all morning. Her voice held a note of caution.

Durga was now about eleven. She was thin and darker than Apu. Glass bangles clinking on her arms, a none-too-clean sari and windswept dry hair flying any which way—that was Durga. On her finely shaped face her eyes shone large like her brother's.

'What is it?' asked Apu, jumping off the veranda in front of their house and coming up to her. Durga held a half coconut shell in her hands. She lowered it to show Apu its contents—slivers of tender green mango before the seed had hardened. Then, in an undertone, 'Is Ma back from the ghat yet?'

'No,' said Apu, shaking his head.

'Can you fetch me a bit of oil and some salt?' she asked him secretively. 'I'll pickle these . . .'

'Wherever did you get them from, Didi?' Apu was delighted.

'They were lying on the ground just under the sindurkauto tree in Potli's garden. Now get me a pinch of salt and some oil, will you?'

'But Ma will give it to me if I so much as bring down the oil pot from the shelf,' replied Apu, scared. 'I'm still wearing last night's clothes . . . haven't bathed yet.'

'Run and get it, fast. It will be a while before she's back; she's gone to wash the clothes with fuller's earth. Hurry up!'

'The shell,' said Apu. 'Give me the shell. I'll pour it into the shell. You stand by the backdoor and keep a lookout.'

'Mind you don't spill any oil on the floor. Better be careful, otherwise Ma'll know for sure: you're such a good for nothing.'

When Apu came out of the house Durga took the coconut shell from him and expertly got the mix of oil and salt into the mango slices. 'Here, put out your hand—'

'Didi, are you going to eat all the rest yourself?'

'Does this look like *all* that much to you? There's not that much. Okay, you can have a couple more. Mmm, looks really good! Do you think you can get us a nice chilli? I'll give you an extra slice if you do.'

'But how shall I get to the chillies, Didi? They're right up on the shelf. I can't even reach it!'

'Don't bother; I'll get some more mangoes later in the day. You know that tree by the pond at Potli's—there's lots and lots of budding mangoes that'll fall off in the afternoon sun.'

The backdoor opened with a sharp clang and Sarbojoya was heard calling out, 'Dugga . . . O Dugg-a-a-a!'

'That's Ma calling—quick, go and see what's up. Finish it up over there . . . no, wait, you've got grains of salt all over your mouth. Wipe them away first.'

Durga heard her mother call out yet again, but there was no way she could reply for her mouth was quite full. She began furiously devouring the slices of pickled mango. When she found that she still had many left she hid behind the trunk of the jackfruit tree and started to gobble up the rest. Apu stood beside her frantically swallowing his share, for there was no time to chew. As he ate, he smiled a guilty smile at his sister. Durga tossed the now empty shell right into the jungly thicket by their house. 'You little monkey,' she said to her brother, 'why don't you wipe your face clean—there is salt all over your face even now!'

Then, putting on a most innocent expression, she entered the house. 'What is it, Ma?' she asked.

'And where had you gone a-wandering, may I know?' asked Sarbojoya. 'How am I to manage everything on my own! Such a big girl, but not a bit of help do I get out of you with the household chores. All you can do is spin around like a top, skipping all over the neighbourhood, tasting this and that—and where's that monkey gone?'

'I'm hungry, Ma,' announced Apu, appearing suddenly.

'Now hold on, let me take a breather. You're eternally hungry, the two of you: am I to be kept busy running errands for you? O, Dugga, go and check on the calf, will you? It's been lowing away.'

A little later when she sat down in the veranda in front of the kitchen to cut up a cucumber for the children, Apu flopped down next to her. 'Ma, do take out some more of that white stuff out of the cucumber, it sticks in my mouth,' he said.

Durga spread out her palm to get her share and asked a little hesitantly, 'Isn't there any more of the rice fry, Ma?'

'Oh, it's impossible . . . all those tart mangoes have set my teeth on edge—' began Apu. He stopped abruptly when he saw Durga frowning and winking at him.

'Where did you get mangoes from?' asked his mother.

Apu was afraid to tell the truth; he looked questioningly at his sister wondering what to reply.

Sarbojoya turned to her daughter and demanded, 'So, you'd gone out again?'

Durga paled. 'Ask him—I was just there by the jackfruit tree . . . and then, just as you called—'

Fortunately, the conversation was cut short by the entry of the milkwoman Shorno. She had come to milk their cow.

'Go catch the calf,' said Sarbojoya to her daughter, 'it's been crying away. Such a young thing too.' To the milkwoman she said, 'Shonno, what makes you so late? Do you think that calf'll live if you're going to be so late . . . It's been tied up for ages in this blazing sun.'

Apu followed his sister out to watch the cow being milked. As soon as he stepped into the outer courtyard Durga landed him a smart blow on his back. 'You wretch! Monkey!' She made faces at him and mimicked him, '"All those tart mangoes have set my teeth on edge . . ." You think I'm ever going to give you any! Not one mango will you get from me. Rubbish! I'm just going to get some more mangoes that've fallen off from that other tree in Potli's garden . . . such big-seeded ones they are and sweet as jaggery too. And I shall pickle them. Don't you think you'll get any—not one lick for you. Dumbo! No brains at all!'

Harihar came back from work later that afternoon. He was now employed as a rent collector at Annada Ray's. 'Have you seen Apu?' he asked his wife.

'He's indoors, sleeping.'

'And Dugga?'

'She trotted off right after her meal. You think she ever stays home? Those two mouthfuls of food are all that tie her home. She will be back only when she's hungry. Must be prowling around in someone's orchard or the other . . . and in this April sun too. Bound to run up a fever again. A grown-up girl, but she'll not hear a thing or listen to anything I say . . .'

7

Summer afternoons

Some distance away from Apu's house stood a huge pipal tree. You could only see its top if you looked through the window along the corridor or from the raised terrace in front of the house. Apu would find himself gazing at it from time to time. And whenever he did so, he was reminded of a distant land, far far away. He never quite knew exactly what place it was . . . somewhere . . . where lived the princes of his mother's fairy tales. A certain joy and wonder would stir his childish mind. And yet, at the very moment when his imagination had flown him away into this faraway land, he began to miss his mother most intensely. It was so intriguing! As though he would suddenly recall that the land to which he was going was a place without his mother; and right away, he would long to be by her side. It had happened so, many a time. A kite would be flying high above in the skies growing smaller and smaller and smaller still as it flew over the tall palm in Neelu's garden before disappearing into the boundless sky. As soon as the speck of the flying kite disappeared, Apu would bring his gaze back to the earth, and then find himself running towards the kitchen veranda and in one bound holding his mother in a tight embrace. 'Just look at the boy!' his mother would exclaim, 'Let go! Let go of me! Can't you see I'm cooking and my hands are messy? Let go of me, my darling . . . See, I'm frying these prawns just for you—you love them, don't you? Don't be naughty and let go.'

Some afternoons, after they have had their meal, his mother lies down on the ground spreading out one end of her sari and reads in a singsong voice verses from the poet Kashidas' rendering of the Mahabharata. A white-breasted kite's shrill cry is heard from the top of the coconut tree near their house. Apu, sitting beside his mother by the open window, practises writing his alphabet while listening with all his heart and soul to her reciting from the Mahabharata. He becomes wholly absorbed in the world of the epic, especially when they come to the battle of Kurukshetra. The day draws to a close. His mother is up and about to finish her household chores. Apu comes out to the veranda and gazes at the distant pipal. Karna is standing somewhere in that direction—beyond the tree, beneath the open sky . . . he is still struggling desperately to lift up with both his hands his sunken chariot wheel trapped in the mud . . . with both his hands he struggles every day with the chariot wheel . . .

On other days as he listened to the Mahabharata, Apu felt that there was too little about the war in the poem. He found a way to make up for this lack and to experience for himself the business of war. Picking up a length of split bamboo as if it was his weapon, he stalked the enclosure near the bamboo copse behind his house as he declaimed: 'And then Drona released ten arrows at one go, but Arjuna released two hundred. And then, what a mighty battle it was . . . such a battle! The air turned dark with arrows. And then, Arjuna—he leapt off his chariot armed with his shield and sword! And then, a terrible battle began. Came Duryodhona, came Bhima . . . the sky turned black with arrows and nothing could be seen!'

It was the end of April, a hot summer's day. By the edge of the jungle where lie the ruins of their uncle Neelmoni Ray's abandoned house, Guru Drona is deep in trouble. Arjuna's chariot, flying its Hanuman banner, is almost upon him. A mere blink of an eye stands between him and Arjuna's terror-arousing Gandiva bow which is about to be let loose on him. The dreaded super weapon, the brahmastra, will be released any moment now. From the Kuru side rise cries of despair and lament—

'What *are* you up to, Apu?' an amused voice from the other side of the jungle cut through the silent afternoon.

Apu found his sister standing and watching him from the jungle of sheora bushes with their zigzagging branches; she was giggling at his antics. When their eyes met, she said, 'You madcap, whatever are you muttering away all by yourself and flinging about your arms and walking this way and that!'

She ran up to him to plant an affectionate kiss on his soft cheeks. 'You are really mad! What *were* you doing?' she demanded.

A shamefaced Apu tried to ward off her questions, 'Come on, was I really muttering! No . . . no . . .'

When Durga had finally stopped laughing at him she said, 'Now, come with me,' and holding him by his hand she led him into the woods, only stopping when they had come to a particular spot.

'Do you see how many nonas have ripened on that tree?' She was pointing to the longish fruits that looked like custard apples. 'How do you think we can get them down?'

'Ooh! So many of them, Didi! Can't we get hold of a split cane to bring them down?'

'Why don't you run home and bring the hooked pole? I'm sure it'll do the job.'

'You wait here for me, and I'll get it,' said Apu, darting off. But after he came back with the hooked pole, though they tried their hardest, they couldn't bring down more than five of the nonas. It was an unusually tall tree and try as she might, Durga couldn't get the hooked end to touch the topmost branch which had the best fruits.

'Let's go back home today with whatever we've got. We'll bring Ma along with us on our way to the bathing ghat. It's sure to be within Ma's reach. Here, give me the nonas; you take the hooked pole . . . How about putting on a nose-ring?' added she, as she began tearing off the white buds of the or-kalmi creeper that flowered all over the low bushes surrounding them. 'Come closer, and I'll put a nose-ring on you,' she said to her brother. Durga liked putting on these little white flowers of the or-kalmi, pretending they were nose-rings. She would hunt for them in the jungles and if she found one, she always put one on her nose; in the past she had put them on Apu's nose as well. Apu however, didn't really enjoy doing this. Now, he wished to say that he could do without a nose-ring. But he kept quiet because he was afraid of his sister. He didn't in the least wish to annoy her because it was she who hunted around in wastelands and brought him the pick of delicious nonas, sweet-sour jujubes, tart hog plums and juicy purple plums when the rains came. She managed to lay her hands on all sorts of things, even those that they were forbidden to eat. So, right or wrong, he didn't dare disobey his sister.

Durga broke off a bud and using the sticky white fluid that oozed out of the stalk, stuck the bud on one of his nostrils. She wore one herself. Then chucking him fondly under the chin she turned his face towards herself. 'Let's see how it looks. Oh! That's sweet. Come, let's show it to Ma.'

'No, no, Didi,' Apu tried to protest, quite ashamed of his nose-ring.

'Why, let's go. Don't take it off: it looks good.'

When they got home Durga laid down all the nonas by the kitchen door.

'Where did you get them, dear?' Sarbojoya was busy cooking but she was very pleased at the sight of the fruits.

'They were growing by the litchi jungle . . . loads of them.

Will you come with us and get some tomorrow? They are so ripe too, flaming red like sindur.' Then, moving aside to reveal Apu standing behind her with his nose-ring, she said, 'Look, Ma!'

'Goodness me! Now who can that be?' said Sarbojoya with a laugh. 'Can't recognize this person . . .'

Apu hurriedly took off the bud that hung from his nose. 'It's Didi,' he said bashfully, 'she made me wear it—'

'Come Apu, come on!' broke in Durga, 'I hear the dugdugi rattling away . . . must be the monkey-man with his drum. Come quick.' In a trice Durga had run out of the house and close behind her, Apu.

But it wasn't the monkey-man after all who appeared in the path ahead of them. It was Chinibash, the sweetmaker from the neighbouring village, on his rounds to sell the sweets he was carrying on his head. Chinibash walked past Harihar's outer door without any attempt to enter the house. He knew the people of this house never bought anything from him. Nevertheless, when he saw Durga and Apu standing at the door he did ask, 'Want any?'

Apu looked at his sister. But she shook her head at Chinibash and said, 'No.'

Bhubon Mukherjee was a wealthy man: he had about half a dozen stacks of paddy heaped up in his compound. His wife had died a long time ago; his widowed sister-in-law, who was called Shejo bou (or the middle daughter-in-law) by all, ran the household. She was over forty and was renowned for her sharp tongue and quick temper.

Shejo bou bought an array of confectionaries as offerings for her Ganga puja—white puffy murki, delicate crunchy batasha, and lots of sandesh, all of which she stored in a freshly shined brass bowl. She then bought sweets for the children—Bhubon Mukherjee's and her own, who were all milling around Chinibash. When she saw that Durga, and along with her Apu, had followed Chinibash into their courtyard, she gave her son Sunil a little shake on his shoulder and said quite loudly, 'Why can't you get up on the veranda and eat your sweets? I've bought the offerings for the puja—can't let any of it get dirty.'

Chinibash had now picked up his wares and was setting off for another house with the tray on his head.

'Come, Apu,' said Durga, 'let's go to Runu's.'

The two had barely gone past the outer door when Shejo bou made a face and exclaimed, 'Can't abide them! The girl's such a greedy creature! Got a home, haven't you—why don't you sit at home and buy something and eat it there! No, they must run from house to house. Like mother, like brats!'

As they came out of Bhubon Mukherjee's house, Durga tried to comfort her brother: 'Nothing so great about that Chinibash's sweets. Just wait and see, I'm going to get four paise from Baba for the Chariot festival—two for you and two for me. And we'll buy heaps of sugar-coated rice . . .'

Apu thought about this and after a while, he asked, 'Didi, how long is it before the festival?'

8

Dugga didi

About a month later . . .
Sarbojoya mixed some rice with milk and sat down to feed her son. 'Now, open your mouth . . . It's too bad that I can't feed you either sweets or anything special—only plain milk and rice . . . Look at the boy: puckering up his face every time he sits down to eat. How will he live if it goes on like this?'

Durga was making an entry after wandering about goodness knows where. Her feet were covered in dust and a strand of rough hair, almost four inches high, stood up straight and stiff like a banner above her forehead. She didn't much care about playing with the neighbourhood children but was forever outdoors exploring the countryside on her own. She knew exactly where and when the first of the tiny violet-pink bainchi berries ripened, which were the sweetest jujubes growing in the middle of this or that clump of bamboos, and when the first tiny mango would have blossomed in somebody's orchard.

Durga gave her mother a guilty look as she came in.

'So, you're home, finally,' said Sarbojoya. 'The rice is done: kindly come in and do me a favour by eating your food before you set off again for wherever it is you wish to go. It's May and all the other girls are busy sewing rag-quilts or performing the rituals for worshipping Shiva, but this one—such a big growing girl—she's out the whole day, got wheels on her feet! Left the house at daybreak 'most, and she puts in an appearance now, when it's late afternoon. And look at the state of her hair—not a drop of oil to get rid of the tangles; never runs a comb through it, I'm sure—' Before Sarbojoya was quite done, something else happened.

First came Bhubon Mukherjee's sister-in-law; behind her came her daughter and nephew Satu and, behind them, a tail of four or five children. The whole lot walked right into the courtyard. Shejo bou looked neither to the left or right, nor did she deign to speak with anyone. She marched up the steps to the veranda, turned to her nephew and commanded him, 'Get it out! Fetch her doll's box. And we shall take a look.' Before any of the inmates could say a word, Tunu and Satu had both run inside, got out Durga's little tin box and had set it on the platform. Tunu opened the box and after a bit of searching fished out a string of beads. 'My necklace, Ma!' she exclaimed. 'You remember, she came to play with us the other day—that's when she stole it.' Satu, who in the meantime had been examining another corner of the box, now held up a couple of mango seeds: 'Look, Auntie, she's got these from our special sonamukhi tree!'

Everything happened so fast and the visitors' movements seemed so mystifying that the people of the house were nonplussed and struck dumb. Finally, Sarbojoya found her voice. 'What is it? What has happened, Auntie?' she asked anxiously, coming out from the kitchen to the courtyard.

'What's up, indeed! Look at what she's up to! Your daughter filched this necklace from Tunu's box when she came over to our place the other day. The girl's gone crazy looking for it these last few days. Then Satu came and told her, "I've just seen your beads in Dugga didi's box." What a thing and half! That daughter of yours is quite something. A thief— an honest to goodness thief—that's what she is! And look at *this*: will she ever let a mango ripen on the tree! Stole all the budding mangoes and hid them away in her box.'

Durga, standing with her back to the boundary wall, stiff and sweating, heard herself suddenly being charged of not one but two thefts.

'Did you bring the beads from their place?' Sarbojoya asked her daughter.

Before Durga could come up with an answer, Shejo bou cried out, 'What would I be coming here for if she hadn't— you think I'm lying? Look at the mangoes, I tell you! Don't you know these are sonamukhi mangoes! Is that a lie too?'

'Not at all, Auntie,' Sarbojoya said in embarrassment, 'I never said that you were lying. I was only asking her.'

With a dramatic flourish of her hands Shejo bou shot back, 'Ask her or do whatever you will, but let me tell you that girl's not a straight one. Mark my words: if she's honing her skills at such an early age, you will find out soon enough what she'll do by and by. Come on Satu, let's get going and don't forget those mango seeds . . .'

Shejo bou departed with her retinue after this speech.

Stung by the insult, in sorrow Sarbojoya's eyes filled with tears. Turning to Durga she grasped her dry and tangled hair with one hand and with the other, which still had rice and milk on it, she began raining blows on her daughter's back and slapping her cheeks and cursing her. 'A monster that's turned up from goodness knows where; I'll be quit of this shame only when you die. But this one won't even *die*—else I would've had a moment's rest. Get out, get out of this house this minute.'

Durga fled from the backdoor, terrorized by the slapping and beating that went on till the last minute. A few strands of her unkempt hair still dangled from Sarbojoya's fingers.

Apu who was midway through his meal, had been staring in amazement at all that had happened. He did not know whether his sister had really stolen the beads and brought them home—he had never seen the string of beads before. But he knew for certain that the mango seeds were not stolen. His sister had taken him to Tunu's the evening before and she had picked up the sonamukhi mangoes that were lying on the ground in their garden. And ever since Durga had kept telling him, 'We'll pickle those delicious sonamukhi mangoes, right?' But unfortunately their mother had been at home for inconveniently long stretches and they had been unable to carry out the plan. Such a precious find of his Didi's had been snatched away and on top of it his Didi had been beaten up so badly by Ma! He was very angry with his mother for tearing his sister's hair. That one strand of his sister's hair standing up stiff and blowing in the wind always filled him with an inexplicable tenderness for her. It somehow made him feel that Didi had no one of her own—as though she had come all alone from some far-off place and had no one for a friend. He wanted only to find some way of taking away all her sorrows, of fulfilling all her desires and needs. He wouldn't let his Didi suffer even one little bit.

After his meal Apu sat down to study for fear of his mother. But every now and then his thoughts would race outdoors. As soon as the afternoon waned he went looking in all the possible places his sister might be: Runu, Potli, Neda—he visited all their homes in turn . . . but Didi was nowhere to be found.

'Auntie, have you seen my Didi?' he asked of Rajkrishna Palit's wife, who was returning with water from the ghat. 'She hasn't had a meal this afternoon, she's not eaten a thing and Ma's given her a terrible beating—she's run off somewhere after the beating; have you seen her, Auntie?'

On his way home past the bamboo thicket he wondered, would she be sitting somewhere inside the thicket? He stopped and searched everywhere for her. He finally went home but peeping in through the backdoor could see no one. His mother must have gone to the ghat to wash clothes.

At Bhubon Mukherjee's, the children were having a great time playing hide and seek. Ranu came running towards him, 'Apu's come!' she called out happily to her brother, 'He'll be on our side. Come, Apu.'

Apu freed his hand from hers and said, 'I shan't play today, Ranudi, have you seen Didi?'

'Dugga? No, I haven't seen her,' said Ranu. 'You think she might be at the Bakul-tala?'

Oh, he had quite forgotten about the Bakul-tala. It was true that Durga was often to be found there. So from Bhubon Mukherjee's he set off towards Bakul-tala. It was getting dark. The bakul tree stood there spreading its branches afar in different directions looking like a vast and tangled shadow. It was pitch dark beneath the tree. Not a soul in sight. Would she be behind the tree? 'Didi, O Didi, Didi-i-i-i,' he called out.

All one could hear were a few egrets rustling their wings on the dark form of the tree. Apu gazed up nervously. On his way back home he came to a sudden halt. There was the gaub tree again! To walk under this gaub tree alone in the dark! It was terrifying! His hair stood on end. He did not know *why* he was so scared of walking beneath this particular tree.

Apu turned back after he had spent some time staring at the massive gaub tree with its outspread branches. There was another route he could take to go home. This was a roundabout way through the courtyard of Potli's home, but at least he would escape the unknown terrors that this place held for him.

Potli's grandmother was enjoying the early evening breeze as she sat on the raised veranda of their house telling stories to the children clustered around her. Potli's mother was in the kitchen, busy cooking. In the courtyard by the cucumber frame stood fisherwoman Bidhu pressing for her dues.

'I've been searching for my Didi, Granny . . . I'm on my way from Bakul-tala . . .' began Apu.

'But Dugga's just left for home . . .' said she, 'only a moment ago. Run and catch up with her—most likely she's yet not reached home.'

He set off at a run for home. Potli's sister Raji was calling out to him, 'Apu, do come tomorrow morning. We've drawn new lines and squares for our game behind the mortar by the neem tree, and tell Dugga too—'

He was about to enter his home when he braked to a halt. Durga was screaming as she ran out of the house chased by her mother, who was hitting out at her with something she held in her hand. Durga fled along the path which led to the gaub tree while her mother shouted out from the door at the fleeing figure: 'Go away, get out, go away for ever. Never come back home again. A menace gone! Good riddance! I'll see you to the Chhatim-tala.' Chhatim-tala was where the dead bodies were taken for cremation. Apu felt as though he was turning into stone, frozen and heavy, unable to move a step. His mother was now picking up the earthen lamp from one of the rooms. He had barely tiptoed indoors when his mother looked at him and said, 'Where have you been roaming around at such a late hour, may I know? You've only just recovered from a fever.'

He was bursting with questions. Why was Didi being beaten again? Where had she been all this time? What did she eat in the afternoon? Had she again brought home something she had stolen? But he was too scared to say a word; like a clockwork toy he did everything his mother asked him to and entered the room to study. Then, fearfully turning up the wick a little bit, he spread out his little library and sat down before it. Although he was still studying the Third Primer, his collection included two heavy tomes of English books (he didn't know what they were), a list of medicinal plants, a tattered copy of narrative verse—*Dashu Ray's Panchali*—an ancient almanac of the 1890s and other such books. He had acquired each of them from different sources and although he couldn't quite read them he had to go through them at least once every day. Today he sat staring at the wall for a while. Then, once again turning up the wick, he sat down with the tattered *Dashu Ray*. He had begun flipping through the pages absent-mindedly when Sarbojoya came in with a bowl of milk and said, 'Drink this up.'

Without a murmur Apu tilted the bowl and started drinking. On other days it was almost impossible to make him drink his milk. But he put down the bowl after he had drunk only a bit. 'What's that now?' said Sarbojoya, 'You must drink it all up . . . how will you grow big and strong if you drink so little?' Apu picked up the bowl a second time without any fuss. Sarbojoya saw that he held the bowl to his lips but was not sipping any milk. He was holding on to the bowl with trembling fingers. When he had held it for quite long he suddenly put it down and, turning to his mother, let out a choked sob.

'What has happened now?' asked Sarbojoya in astonishment. 'What is it? Have you bitten your tongue or what?' His mother had scarcely finished speaking when his anguished sobs burst through his barriers of fear, 'I'm hurting for Didi, Ma!' Sarbojoya was quiet for a while before she came up close to her son and soothing him with gentle strokes of her palm said calmly, 'Don't cry, my darling, don't cry in that way. Must be at Potla's or Neda's—where else would she go in the dark? She's such a naughty creature! Went out in the afternoon and not a trace of her all day, not eating not bathing, sat somewhere that side of the village at the Palits' garden and had some of their raw mango and their roseapples . . . I'll send for her right away, hush now, don't you cry—you'll fall ill again, don't!'

She wiped away her son's tears with her sari-end and raised the bowl to make him drink the remaining milk, 'Now my darling, open your mouth, that's a dear. Your father will go and get her as soon as he's back. What a madcap you are . . . where did this crazy child of mine come from . . . another sip, that's right . . .'

It was late at night. Apu and Durga were lying on the bed in the north room. Beside Apu was an empty space where his mother would sleep. She was still cleaning up in the kitchen. His father had finished his dinner and was now smoking his hookah in the next room. He had hunted out Durga and brought her back after he had got home.

Durga had not said a word to anyone since her return. She was lying down quietly after her meal. Apu put his hand on his sister and asked her, 'Didi, what did Ma hit you with this evening? Did she pull out your hair?'

Not a sound came from Durga's lips.

He asked again, 'Are you mad at me, Didi? But I didn't do anything!'

'Nothing?' said Durga very slowly. 'Then how did Satu get to know that the bead necklace was in my box?'

Apu got up from the bed as he excitedly protested against her suspicion. 'Honestly, Didi, I swear, I didn't show him the necklace. I didn't even *know* it was there in your box. Satuda came over last afternoon and we were playing throw with that big red ball of his, and then you know, Didi, Satuda had opened your doll's box and was looking at something, and I told him, "Don't touch Didi's box, Didi scolds me if I do,"—that's when he must have seen . . .' A little later he gently stroked his sister and said, 'It's hurting a lot, isn't it Didi? Where did Ma hit you?'

'Ma gave me a blow on my ear,' said Durga. 'It bled a lot, and it's still throbbing. Over here . . . see, you can still feel it! Here . . .'

'Here? Ahh, yes! It's cut. Shall I put some oil from the lamp on it, Didi?'

'Let it be. We'll go to the Palits' garden tomorrow afternoon, okay? Such soft ripe star apples there are. So-o-o big—don't tell anyone. You and I shall go there secretly . . . I plucked and ate two of 'em this afternoon—sweet as jaggery they were!'

9

Lemon leaf 'n berry

Suddenly, towards late afternoon, darkness fell and a monstrous pre-monsoon storm broke loose. Clouds had been gradually massing in the sky for some time now, but the storm seemed to come unawares. The wind smashed into the bamboos in front of Apu's home with such force that they toppled over the other side of the wall, making their house look strangely empty. Leaves of the bamboo and the jackfruit tree, dust and bits of straw came whirling into their courtyard filling it up in seconds. Durga sped out of the house to pick up falling mangoes and Apu ran after his sister.

'Faster!' urged Durga as she raced along, 'You go to the sindurkauto trees and I'll head for the sonamukhi side. Run!'

The dust was everywhere, swirling and covering everything. Huge branches had snapped and twisted in the storm—the trees looked stripped and bare. The wind whistled and screamed through the gaps in the trees. Dry twigs, bits of parched bamboo sheaths and chaff flew all around them; the pointed ends of the spiny bamboo leaves spun upwards into the sky twisting and turning in the wind. The storm brought in its wake vast numbers of feathery white flowers of the kukshima, their filaments streaming in the wind. The storm was deafening, drowning all other sounds.

When he got to Sonamukhi-tala Apu was beside himself in excitement, hopping about, screaming out to his sister, 'This way, Didi, come here, there's one falling here, Didi! . . . There goes another!' In his enthusiasm there was more shouting than picking up of falling mangoes. The storm grew fiercer. Soon it was impossible to hear a mango fall for it got drowned in the roar of the storm. Even if you did hear a fruit hit the ground it was impossible to locate exactly where the sound had come from. Durga rapidly gathered eight or more mangoes. Apu with all his prancing and shouting had managed to get only two. But he was showing them off to his sister with great delight: 'Look how big this one is, Didi! Oh! Another one's fallen over there . . .'

Just then voices were heard. The children from Bhubon Mukherjee's were heading towards them in a group, evidently with the same thought of gathering storm-blown mangoes. 'Look, look,' shouted Satu, 'there's Dugga didi and Apu picking up mangoes!' The whole lot swooped down on brother and sister. 'Why have you come to our orchard to pick up mangoes?' demanded Satu. 'Didn't Ma forbid you the other day? Let's see how many you've got!' He turned to his cousin and said, 'See how many of the sonamukhis she's gathered, Tunu! Get away from our garden, Dugga didi, else I'll tell Ma.'

'Why are you chasing them away, Satuda?' said Ranu, 'Let them pick up some of the fallen mangoes, and we'll gather some too.'

'If you let her stay, she's sure to pick up every single one of them. Why should she come to *our* garden? Go away, Dugga didi, I shan't let you stay in our orchard.'

Had it been some other time Durga might not have accepted defeat so easily, but she didn't dare start a quarrel so soon after the thrashing she had got from her mother. So she quickly gave way and called out despondently to her brother, 'Let's go, Apu.' Then suddenly, pretending to be very excited, she said to him, 'You know, Apu, let's go to that special place of ours . . . much I care if they don't let us stay here. They're so much bigger there, anyway. We'll have such fun picking up the mangoes there. Come on, let's go.'

'Why did you have to drive them away—you're really very selfish, Satuda!' Ranu was pained by the helpless look in Durga's eyes.

Apu had not quite understood the situation. When they had gone past the fence, he said, 'And where are the big ones, Didi? Near Putu's home?'

Durga hadn't yet decided exactly where the special place was. She thought for a moment and said, 'Let's go to the garden by the Gor Pond; there are some big trees thataway.'

The pond was some distance away. It meant a good fifteen

minutes of brisk walking through jungle and orchards, past ancient mango and jackfruit trees tangled with creepers and almost impenetrable bushes that covered the ground. No one lived there as it was far from the village proper and certainly no one came to such places to gather mangoes. Tough strands of gulancha creepers hung from the trees like thick coils of rope. It was not at all easy to find fallen mangoes in the thorny undergrowth. Besides, the storm clouds had darkened the sky so much that it was hardly possible to see clearly. But the determined Durga was not going to give up and after a great deal of scouring around she did manage to find about ten mangoes. Suddenly she cried out, 'Apu! Here comes the rain!'

As it began raining it looked for a while that the storm had let up a bit. The smell of wet earth filled the air as thick fat drops of rain began to fall on the leaves of the myriad trees around them.

'Let's get under this tree, then we won't be wet,' said Durga.

In a minute however the rain began to pour in torrents and turned everything misty. The force of the raindrops tore the leaves off trees and they landed on the freshly drenched earth which was sending off its very own scent. Now the storm which had calmed down turned fierce again. The tree beneath which Durga and Apu had taken shelter might have protected them from the downpour, but the east wind blew stinging sheets of rain in their direction. They were stuck, and far from home. 'Didi,' said Apu in a scared voice, 'it's raining ever so hard now . . .'

'Come closer,' said Durga to her brother. Drawing him

near her she covered him with a part of her sari. 'It won't go on like this,' she sought to comfort him, 'the rain's about to stop. Isn't it good that it's raining though—now we can go back to Sonamukhi-tala, isn't that so?'

Then the two of them began reciting at the top of their voices, against the sound of the storm:

Lemon leaf 'n berry
rain do not tarry

Crash! A blinding flash of lightning sliced the dark sky that hovered ominously from one end to the other of the immense wasteland. 'Ohh, Didi!' said Apu, clutching on to his sister with all his might.

'Don't be afraid . . . say Rama . . . Rama . . . Rama . . . Rama . . . *lemon leaf 'n berry . . . rain do not tarry . . . lemon leaf 'n berry . . . rain do not tarry . . .'*

Apu had shut his eyes in fear. Durga glanced up, dry mouthed. Was the lightning going to strike again? The gourds of wild dhundul flowers swayed atop the trees, buffetted by the rain. Apu's teeth were chattering in the cold. Durga enfolded him completely in her arms and as a last resort, kept reciting the verse almost as if it were a spell to keep the storm at bay, '. . . *lemon leaf 'n berry . . . rain do not tarry . . . lemon leaf 'n berry . . . rain do not tarry . . .'*

Her voice was trembling.

It was dusk. The storm and the rain had died down somewhat. Sarbojoya waited at the outer door for her children. Rajkrishna Palit's daughter, Ashalata, was heading towards the ghat, her feet squelching and splashing in the mud and water.

'My dear, did you see Durga and Apu by the ghat?' Sarbojoya asked.

'No, Auntie, I haven't. Why, where have they gone? What a storm that was, enough to set the frogs croaking!' she added with a laugh.

'They ran off just before the storm started—going to pick up mangoes they said; they've not been back since. Such wild weather we've had . . . and it's getting on to be evening. Where could they be?'

Sarbojoya went in, full of worries. She was wondering what she should do when Durga burst in, soaked to the skin, a ripe old coconut in her hand. Behind her came Apu dragging a huge palm strand that had dried and fallen off the tree.

'What a sight you are!' their mother exclaimed, 'Dripping with water! Where were you when it was pouring?' She drew her son to her and stroked his hair, 'Soaking wet!' Then she noticed what her daughter was holding. 'Where did you get the coconut from, Dugga?' She sounded quite happy.

'Shhh!' cried out the two of them in unison. 'Tunu's mother is on her way to the orchard . . . there—she's gone . . .! You know that coconut tree just on the other side of the fence . . . this was lying on the ground next to it. She was on her way just as we were leaving.'

'She must have seen Apu for sure, and she may've spotted me too,' said Durga. She whispered excitedly to her mother,

'It was right at the foot of the tree. I'd no idea it was there at first. We went to Sonamukhi-tala to look for mangoes . . . you know, in case the storm had brought some down, and then I saw this palm strand. "Pick it, Apu!" I said to him, "Ma needs a broom and we can make a really nice one out of this." And right then I spotted this—' she turned her shining eyes to the coconut in her hand. 'A biggish one, isn't it, Ma?'

'And I picked up the strand and dashed away,' said a grinning Apu, gesticulating with his hands.

'Yes, it is quite a big one. Put it away in the corner there, just beneath the thatch. I'll have to wash it first. Now wash your feet, both of you, and come up to the veranda. I want to get these wet clothes off you.'

Some time later, Sarbojoya went to Bhubon Mukherjee's house to draw water from their well. As she approached the outer door she could hear Shejo bou screaming her head off: 'The orchard's not to be had for free, I tell you—had to shell out *loads* of money to rent it. But with all the creatures who come raiding it, you think I'll ever get to see a blade of green grass on it! The rain's stopped, I say to myself, I'll do a round of the garden—and then I see her, and right before my eyes she picks up this *huge* coconut and scampers away. O Lord, are you going to let such enemies get away! Let 'em go to ruin, let 'em not have any coconut! I pronounce these words at this hour of dusk . . .'

Sarbojoya stood frozen at the outer door. She saw before

her the tender faces of her children and thought, 'What if the curse affects them? She's capable of spewing such venom! What should I do?' She almost fainted at the thought of the harm being wished on her children. She didn't enter the Mukherjee home, but putting the little bucket and the pot in the crook of her arm, walked back home in fear.

'But what if I return the coconut?' she brooded on the way, 'Would the curse still work? But why would it? If one is returning what belongs to them, surely the curse won't work?'

As soon as she stepped into the courtyard she said to her daughter, 'Dugga, take the coconut to Satu's and give it back to them.' Apu and Durga stared at their mother in great surprise.

'Right now?' asked Durga.

'Yes, give it back right away. The outer door to their house is open; go now. Tell them that you picked it up from the ground, and that you are now giving it back.'

'Won't Apu come and stand with me . . . it's so dark, Ma. Apu, come with me . . .'

When the children had left, Sarbojoya lit the evening lamp by the sacred tulsi. Draping the sari-end around her neck she bent her head in prayer, 'Dear God, you know that they didn't pick up the coconut out of spite or enmity— let the curse not fall on them. I beg of you God, keep them alive and well. Bless them. Dear God, look upon them with grace, I beg of you.'

10

Guruji

Prasanna Guruji ran a grocery shop from his home, and he ran a school next to the shop. Not much was offered by way of facilities in this school, excepting for the cane.

However, the guardians of his pupils had no less faith than did Guruji on the magical powers of the cane as an instrument of learning. They had assured Guruji that he could wield a free hand with the cane, as long as he didn't actually blind or lame his students. Guruji appeared to follow their request to the letter and it was a miracle that his students remained with their limbs intact.

'Apu, get up! Quick!' said his mother on a cold December morning. Apu lay curled up in his quilt, waiting for the day to get really sunny before he actually got out of bed. 'Wake up, Apu, don't you remember, you're to start school today!' Sarbojoya sat down beside her son to wake him up: 'You will have lots of books and a slate, too . . . now get up and wash your face. Get ready, your father will be along in a moment to drop you off at the school.'

At the sound of the word school, Apu looked at his mother in dismay and disbelief. He believed that only naughty boys who didn't listen to their mother or who fought with their siblings, were the ones sent to school. But *he* had never behaved like that—why then was he being sent to school? He didn't move.

Sarbojoya was back soon, 'Get up, Apu! Wash your face! I'm going to give you a big bundle of puffed rice to take with you to school and you can munch on them on the way. Now get up my darling.' Apu merely let out an exclamation of disbelief. Then he stuck out his tongue and shut his eyes, but showed no signs of stirring.

But finally when his father appeared there was not much he could do; he had to prepare himself for school. He looked mutely at his mother with a hurt expression, his eyes wet with tears. While his mother was tying up the bundle of puffed rice for him he declared, 'I shall never come back home again, just see if I do!'

'Hush, what a thing to say! Never come back home! It isn't good to say such ill-omened words.' She chucked him under the chin and gave him a kiss, 'May you become wise and learned. You must study hard and you are sure to get a wonderful job and earn lots of money. Don't be afraid.' To her husband she said, 'Please tell the Guruji not to scold him—to let him be.'

When they came to the school Harihar said to his son, 'I shall come back later to get you Apu, once school is over. Meanwhile, you must sit and write. Listen to your Guruji and don't be naughty.' When Apu looked back a little later he could see his father's figure gradually disappearing behind the bend in the path. He felt lost, as though he was drowning in a vast ocean. For what seemed ages he sat with his face turned to the ground. Later, when he glanced up timidly, he saw that Guruji was weighing out rock salt for one of his village customers. The bigger boys were seated on their own mats and were reciting something in discordant notes, swaying wildly to a rhythm as they did so. Another boy who looked younger than him, sat with his back to the wall, chewing in a somewhat absentminded way on the leaf strip on which they were supposed to write. And a really big boy with a mole on his face was gazing intently at something beneath the shop platform.

A couple of boys who were seated right in front of him had drawn lines on their slate and were busy doing something, Apu couldn't see what. 'I've put down a cross,' whispered one to the other. 'Here's my nought,' said the other. They went on like that, whispering and putting marks on the slate, all the while throwing quick glances at their teacher who was busy selling goods to his customers. Apu began to spell out words in big letters on his slate. Suddenly— he wasn't sure exactly when—he heard Guruji call out, 'Here you, Foni! What's that you're writing on the slate?' The two boys immediately covered up the slate but it wasn't easy escaping the eagle eyes of their teacher. 'Sateyy! Fetch me Foni's slate,' Guru moshai barked. Before he had quite finished, the big boy with the mole had snatched the slate away and presented it to their teacher who sat on the raised platform of the shop. 'I see. So this is what you've been up to, playing games. Fetch 'em both, Sateyy. Bring 'em up by their ears.'

The sudden snatching away of the slate by the big boy and the panic-stricken expression of the two boys who were now following him reluctantly to Guruji's seat made Apu want to laugh, and a little later he did burst out laughing. For a bit he succeeded in holding back his laughter but soon enough he began to giggle.

'Who is laughing?' called out Guruji. 'Boy, why are you laughing? Do you think you are in a theatre or what?' Apu had no idea of what a theatre might be, but he was scared to death.

'Sateyy!' ordered Guru moshai, 'Pick me a brick from the pile near the tamarind tree. And mind you get a big one.'

Apu stiffened in fear. His throat had dried up completely.

But when the brick was got he found that it hadn't come for him, it was meant for those two boys. Guruji had let him off this time, probably because he was little or perhaps because it was his first day at school.

Guruji usually sat on a palm-leaf mat, leaning against a pole. His well-oiled head had greased a part of the bamboo pole to a shiny glaze. In the late afternoon villagers like Dinu Palit or Raju Ray would come over to the shop for a chat. Apu enjoyed listening to their stories much more than he did doing his studies. Raju Ray would talk about how he had set up a tobacco shop in the Ashadu market. Apu drank it all in, it sounded so interesting . . . to open up the thatched front of one's own little shop and shred the tobacco with a sharp cleaver; then, go down to the river every night and cook a meal of rice and fish curry in a little clay pot—he could imagine all of it . . . and perhaps on some days to read by the dim light of the clay lamp the tattered copy of the Mahabharata they had at home or *Dashu Ray's Panchali* that his father owned, as the rain falls in thick drops in the darkness outside. There is no one, only the frogs croaking away in the pond behind him . . . how wonderful! He would most certainly run a tobacco shop when he was grown up.

But it was on the days when Rajkrishna Sanyal from the far side of the village came to join the group that the conversation would scale fresh heights of imagination. Rajkrishna had an extraordinary capacity for telling a tale, whatever be the story or however trivial the incident. He was possessed with the desire to travel to far-off places— the sea port of Dwarka, the Savitri Hills, Chandranath . . . Moreover, it wasn't enough for him to travel on his own, he took his wife and children with him on every trip and came back having spent every paisa he had. If you saw him sitting comfortably by his family shrine, taking a puff on his hand-held hookah, you would be certain that he was the last of the tribe of well-to-do leisurely householders, the kind who had dug in his roots within the compass of the family temple. But one fine morning you would suddenly find his front door locked and barred and not a stir in the premises. What was up? Sanyal babu had departed for the Vindhya Hills or Chandranath or some such place with his entire family in tow. Nothing would be heard of him for a long time. Then, just as suddenly, the villagers would be startled one afternoon to hear the creaking wheels of the pair of bullock carts bringing the family back to their ancestral home. It was Rajkrishna and his family preparing to enter his house; hired hands would be busy clearing the knee-high jungle of nettles and arjun saplings that now blocked the path to his home.

He would inevitably put in an appearance at the school, walking in long strides and carrying a stout stick in his hands. 'Well, Prasanna, how are things with you?' he would greet Apu's teacher. 'Looks like you've spun quite a web! How many flies have you got this time, huh?'

At the sound of his voice Apu, who had so far been absorbed in memorizing his tables, immediately felt a deep thrill; his face beamed with the promise of more wonderful tales. He would inch closer to where Sanyal babu was settling himself on a palm-leaf mat. His slate and books he would put away to one side as if a holiday had been publicly declared and there was no need to study any more. His large shining eyes would drink up every word of the conversation as though he was a traveller from a drought-stricken land.

On some days the topic would shift to rail travel. How Sanyal babu's wife had great difficulty ascending the Savitri Hills or how he had come to blows with the officiating priest in Nabhi Gaya where he was offering oblations to his ancestors. Then, there was a place where you could buy a wonderfully delicate sweet, Sanyal babu pronounced the name: it was called 'pe-da'. Apu found it a very funny name, but decided that when he was grown up he would buy 'pedas' and eat them. And in some other place, Sanyal babu had seen a fakir who lived beneath a pipal tree. If you gave him a smoke of marijuana, he would be quite happy and ask you, 'What sort of fruit would you be wanting to eat?' And once you had told him the name of the fruit you desired he would point to a nearby tree and say, 'Go and get it from the tree.' And people would indeed find a pomegranate flowering on a mango tree or a cluster of bananas hanging from a guava tree.

'That sort of thing has to do with mantras. An uncle of mine once—' Raju Ray would begin.

'If you are going to be talking about mantras and such matters, let me tell you a story,' Dinu Palit would butt in. 'Not a story, actually, for I've seen it with my own eyes. Had you seen old Budho, the cartman from Beledanga? Died at the ripe age of a hundred and that was some twenty-five years ago. We weren't ever a match for him at arm wrestling—and that's when we were young and he was so old. Anyway, once . . . it happened a long time ago . . . I had just turned twenty and was coming home in a cart from

Chakda where I'd gone for a dip in the Ganga. The cart was Budho's and he was driving it. There was me in the cart, my elder aunt and Ananto Mukherjee's nephew Ram—the one that's now settled in Khulna. By the time we got to Kanshona Field the day was almost gone—Rajkrishna here can tell you what a godforsaken place that was in those times. The path cut through that vast plain, you know, and I had some money on me as well . . . so I got very worried. When we came to the place where there is now a new settlement, guess what happened! Four hefty men, dark as the night, appeared from nowhere it seemed, and they held on—two on each side—to the bamboo staves at the end of the cart. We were struck dumb with terror, just about managed to keep sitting inside the cart, and those four simply held on to the bamboo staves and kept walking along with us, walking along, walking along . . . Budho-driver, he was turning back to glance at them every now and then. And he signals to us not to speak a word. The gang keeps on walking with us. Meanwhile, the cart's almost come up to the police outpost in Nawabganj: you could see the lights of the bazaar and all. Then they say, "Ustad, we're done for— we didn't realize it, please let us go." "That I shan't, you rascals," says old Budho. "I'm going to take the bunch of you to the police and have you chained up." When they had begged and pleaded frantically with him, Budho said, "All right, I'll let you off this time, but never do anything like this again." The four melted into the darkness, but they stooped most respectfully to take the dust of Budho's feet before they left. Seen it with my own eyes! It was a mantra that did it: once they took a hold of the bamboo staves, they were stuck there for ever and there was no way they could let go. There they were, walking along with the cart like someone had nailed them there. So, if we're talking about mantras, huh . . .'

The day comes to an end as the stories flow back and forth. The rosy rays of the setting sun fall slantingly on the green wilderness around the school. A tailorbird with its beak pointing up, sits swinging on the gulancha creepers that hang from the jackfruit and the wild fig trees. The heady smell of the creepers and bushes just outside the schoolroom blends with the scent of the palm-leaf mats and the earthen floor, the bundles of torn books and ink, and above all, the strong smoky tang of the tobacco being cut in the shop.

There is a certain image that will forever linger along the shady paths of this village. It is of a wonderstruck little boy on his way home from school. His books and writing instruments tucked in his arm, his special school-going clothes freshly cleaned with fuller's earth, he trots behind his Didi. His small head crowned with a mop of silky black hair, soft and lovely to stroke, has been combed carefully by his mother. The beautiful big eyes are lost in absorbing the wonders of a world just born, so fresh to him. This is the world he knows, surrounded by trees and bushes, this is where his mother feeds him every day, combs his hair and his sister dresses him with fond tenderness. Once outside the circle of this small familiar world he feels he is stepping into a vast unknown universe where his child's mind cannot find a foothold.

The bamboo grove next to the orchard and the narrow path that ran past it going who knows where ... if you were to follow the path it would lead you past the bamboo grove, to a land of hidden treasures by Sankhari Pond. The force of the rain would have loosened the earth beneath the roots of the giant trees, and the tips and edges of pots filled with gold coins would be peeping through the gaps in the earth. Half hidden in the shadows of wild scrub and the shiny green leaves of wild corm and kalmi creepers the treasure lies ... does any one know quite where?

One day there took place an event in school that opened up a new page in his life. That afternoon there was no visitor, so no stories were being traded; it was study time. Apu was immersed in his primer, *Shishu Bodhak*, when Guruji said to the class, 'Pick up your slates: we shall have a round of dictation.'

Although his teacher was not reading out from a book, Apu soon realized that he wasn't speaking in his own words. It was something Guruji had memorized, just as he himself would recite the rhymed verses from *Dashu Ray's Panchali*.

As he listened to his master he felt he had never heard such a string of beautiful words ever before. Not that he understood every word that was being said, but the unknown words and the melody of the meter seemed marvellous to his young mind. The lilting music of the utterances was all the more enchanting because he could not understand all the words, and the mysterious combination of sound and sense brought him sudden glimpses of an exquisite world.

When he was older and went to a proper school he searched out the same passage that had once been dictated to him . . .

'Here in the middle of Janasthan stands Mount Prasraban whose peaks are forever dressed in the deepest azure of rain-bearing clouds blown continuously by the high winds. Covered by the thick verdure of forests the region of the plateau is cool and delightful. The crystal clear waters of the Godavari unravels at its foot, surging and splashing over rocks as it flows . . .'

Some two years ago, when he had gone with his father and the other villagers to catch a glimpse of the blue-throated bird on Saraswati puja day, he had seen a path cutting its way across the vast field and disappearing into an unknown place. He had stared long and lovingly at this dirt road on both sides of which there was a multitude of unknown birds, trees and plants. He had not been able to fathom where and how far did the strip of a path travel to.

'That is the road through the Sonadanga Field,' his father had told him. 'It goes past Madhabpur, Dasghara and merges with the river ghat of Dhalchit.'

But *he* knew that the path could not stop at Dhalchit—

it went far beyond into the land of the epics, the Ramayana and the Mahabharata. Whenever he looked at the topmost branch of the pipal, he remembered that land, so far far away. While he listened to his teacher's dictation it was this path, seen two years ago, that came to his mind.

Beyond the path, somewhere in the distance, where was Mount Prasraban? Where did the path stop, in which far-off spot? Images from that dream world possessed him in glimmering rosy dusk, when the fragrant bushes cast their mysterious shadows. How far away was it, that world whose peaks are forever dressed in the deepest azure of rain-bearing clouds blown continuously by the high winds . . .?

He would soon grow up and find the place for himself.

11

Aturi Witch

One late afternoon just as Apu was planning to set off for a little walk, his mother called out, 'Where are you going? I've made you some roasted rice and gram, don't go away now, Apu . . . have some right away.'

Apu pretended not to hear. Although he knew that his mother had sat down to roast the stuff specially for him— and it was something he loved—how could he stay back! The game must have warmed up at Neelu's by now. He quickly stepped through the backdoor when he heard his mother say again, 'Are you really going out? Look at that! I hurried back from the ghat to make sure you could have it nice and hot . . . O Apu-u-u-u . . .'

Apu sprinted over to Neelu's. But the crowd of boys had already left; the game was over. 'Come, Apu,' suggested Neelu, 'let's go have a look at that nest of fledglings in South Field.'

Apu was agreeable, so the two headed off to South Field. Just beyond the rice fields the brick road to Nawabganj ran straight from west to east as if slashing the field into two. It was over a mile away from the village. Apu had never come so far away: he felt as though he had been dragged away by Neelu to an unfamiliar world, far removed from his own.

'Let's go home, Neeluda,' he urged his friend a little later. 'Ma's sure to scold me. It will get dark and I won't be able to go home all by myself along that path by the gaub tree.'

Coming back, Neelu lost the way. Finally, after a lot of wandering, they found a track through a big mango orchard; they didn't know who it belonged to. There was still some daylight left, but clouds were already darkening the sky. Suddenly, Neelu stopped in his tracks. He pulled at Apu's elbow and looked ahead fearfully: 'Apu!'

'What is it, Neeluda?' asked Apu, not knowing what had frightened his companion. Then he looked up and saw that the narrow path on which they had been walking had led them right into somebody's courtyard. Ahead of them was a small thatched hut and a golden hog plum tree, with bigger plums than usual. Before he could say anything, Neelu gasped, 'Aturi Witch!'

The blood drained off Apu's face. They were in the home of Aturi the witch! Everyone knew that a fisherboy had been punished with death for daring to pick fruit from that very tree they saw in front of them. She had snatched away his life spirit and tied it up with kochu leaves and sunk it into the water. As soon as the fishes had nibbled on it the poor fellow's desire for a fruit was forever quenched—for this life at least. She could pick up any little boy with a mere look, suck dry every drop of his blood before she let go of him again . . . her wicked doings were known to all. As for the one whose blood had been sucked, the poor fellow would not even know that it had happened, but the moment he reached home he would crumple in a heap and never get up again. How many cold winter nights had he snuggled up to his sister inside a quilt and she had told him these stories and others, until he had stopped her with, 'Don't, Didi, *don't* tell me these stories at night—they really scare me. Why don't you tell the story of the beautiful black-eyed rosy-cheeked princess instead?'

Apu took a few steps forward, almost blinded by fear, to see if there was anyone inside the hut. He froze. Right in front of the bamboo fencing stood none other than Aturi Witch herself observing them; in fact, she appeared to be looking directly at him!

To discover the very person he was so petrified of right in front completely paralysed Apu. He was unable to take a step either forward or backward. Aturi Witch appeared to be frowning. Her dented cheeks and withered jowl seemed to hang even more than usual. Step by step she was approaching them as if she wanted to see them at close quarters. 'I'm trapped,' thought Apu, 'there's no escape.' Whatever be the reason, the witch seemed to be particularly angry with him . . . any moment now and she'd catch hold of his life spirit and imprison it inside a bundle of kochu leaves.

Clearly, whatever was happening was because he had spurned the treat his mother had specially made for him, pretended to be deaf to her appeals. He was about to reap the rewards for being so cruel to his mother. He looked around helplessly and pleaded, 'O Old Auntie, I don't know anything. I shan't do anything any more . . . *please* let me go. I shall never come this way again, let me go today, Old Auntie.'

Neelu was close to bursting into tears, but Apu was so terrified that his eyes were quite dry.

'Why are you afeared of me, li'l ones? Ahh? Why be afeared of me?' Then, believing that she was cracking a joke she said, 'D'you think I'll ketch you li'l boys? Come my dears, come into my home and I'll give you some of my spicy mango powder, tart and sweet . . . come . . .'

Spicy mango powder! The old witch was trying to trick them into going inside. It would be all over with them if they so much as stepped in. This was exactly how witches and demonesses tempted you—wasn't it so in all the stories Ma had told him?

What could he do now? Was there a way out? The old woman drew a step closer to him murmuring as she did so, 'Why be afeared of me, li'l boy! I won't say a thing . . . why be afeared?'

This was it. The end. The instant effect of not listening to his mother. Here was the witch right before him and any moment now she would pluck out his life spirit and imprison it in the kochu leaves. His voice a hoarse whisper, he pleaded as a last resort, 'O, Old Auntie, my mother will weep for me. Don't say anything more to me today. I've never ever come to pluck hog plums from your tree. My Ma will cry . . .' By now he was practically blue with terror. He saw everything around him—the hut, the door, the trees, Neeluda—as if in a mist. There was nothing else but the cruel-looking eyes of Aturi Witch, and somewhere fa-a-a-r away, his mother calling him to have the roasted rice. The next moment his immense fear gave way to desperate courage and letting out an indistinct cry of pure terror he fled for his life, breaking through the bushes of ghetu, rough sheora trees and wild growth of rangchita, running any which way in the gathering darkness. He could hear Neelu running behind him.

The old woman wondered why they had been so afraid. 'Never meant to hit 'em or ketch 'em,' she muttered, 'those li'l critters—why were they so afeared of me this evenin' . . . An' such a dear little boy too . . . whose boy is he?'

12

The railroad

This time when he left home on work, Harihar decided to take his son along with him. 'Doesn't get enough to eat at home. At least he'll get a bit of ghee and milk if he's with me . . . it'll do him good,' was how he put it.

Apu had never left Nishchindipur from the time he was born. The furthest he had gone was up to Gosain Garden, Chalta-tala, Bakul-tala, the riverside; at the most, the brick road leading to Nawabganj—that was as much as he had seen of the world. Sometimes, on a hot summer day he would go to the river ghat with his sister. But now the same little Apu was on his way to the wide world which lay beyond the village. His excitement was so great that he had spent sleepless nights keeping track of the days, watching them pass one after another, until, at last—it was time to go.

The village path took a turn leaving the road to Nawabganj on the right and merged with the dirt road to Ashadu-Durgapur. As soon as they were on the Durgapur road he asked his father, 'Where are the rail lines . . . on which the trains run?'

'Just ahead of us,' was Harihar's reply. 'Come on now; we'll have to cross the tracks anyway.'

Once, their Rangi cow's calf had gone missing. They had combed the village but could not find the calf. Finally, after three days of searching, Durga and Apu had made their way to South Field to see if the calf had strayed that far.

His sister was looking far away, beyond the brick road, towards the mist-hidden fields. 'What do you say, Apu?' she said all of a sudden, 'What if we go take a look at the railroad; shall we, Apu?'

Apu looked at his sister with wondering eyes, 'The railroad—but its so-o-o-o far away. How will we get there? How will you find your way?'

'Far away!' exclaimed his sister. 'Who says it's far away! It's just on the other side of the brick road.'

'If the rail lines are nearby we should be able to spot them, shouldn't we?' said Apu. 'Let's go and find out what they're like, if we can see the lines from the brick road.'

They got on to the Nawabganj road and looked in all directions for the rail lines. 'They must be much further away. Looks like we can't get there. They *are* far away. Can't see a thing . . . If we do go that far, how are we to ever get back,' Durga was thinking out aloud. Her hungry eyes were fixed on some far-off point: she was longing to go but she was also afraid. Finally, with an air of desperation she resolved, 'Let's go, Apu. Let's go and see the railroad—it can't be *that* far away. We'll come back before noon for sure. We might actually get to see a train. And we'll tell Ma that we got late trying to find the calf.'

First they checked to see if anyone had noticed them. Then, when the coast was clear, they quickly clambered down the brick road which was on a raised embankment, and in the hot afternoon sun ran past a series of ponds, ditches, racing southwards. They had been running hard when they had run smack into a big water body, chock-a-block with tangled greens of elephant weed. They had also lost their way: there was not a village in sight, only fields of paddy, marshy land and clumps of cane. It was almost impossible to push through the thick cane jungle and their feet sank into the marshy land. It got so hot that they started sweating furiously although it was winter. Durga's sari was ripped in many places by thorns and several times they had to stop to pluck out thorns from his own feet. A little later, it became difficult to even find the path homewards. The railroad was a distant dream. They waded through the shallow water bodies, crossed the paddy fields and finally, after much struggle, found the brick road almost towards evening. Apu remembered that once they reached home, his sister had to tell a whole heap of lies to wriggle out of a beating.

And now, was it going to be so simple, so easy a matter getting to the railroad? No need to run, no need to lose your way and no scolding, no explaining! After they had gone on for a little while Apu was amazed to see a high road, much like the brick one he knew that led to Nawabganj, cutting right through the fields and snaking its way far far away.

Bits of red brick had been piled up to form a kind of embankment. And on it silvery stakes of iron seemed to have been tied together by lengths of rope. As far as the eyes could see, there were these silver-white stakes and the lengths of rope.

'There, Khoka, that's the railroad,' said his father.

Apu leaped over the gate and scrambled up to the road. He could now get his fill of the railroad. His eyes grew round with wonder. Why were the two lines of iron laid out so ... did they go on forever and forever? Did the train actually run on them? But why? Why did it not go on the road, why did it have to run on the iron lines? Wouldn't the wheels slip and slide? And were those things up there called wires? What was that funny whistling sound they made? Was it because the wires were carrying news from far away? But who was sending the news? And however did they send news? And did the istishun lie in that direction? Or was it this way? His questions fell thick and fast. 'Baba, when will the train come? I want to see the train,' he said to his father.

'How can we stop for the train? It's at least another five hours before a train is due.'

'It doesn't matter, Baba, I've never seen a train. All right, Baba?'

'Now, don't be difficult. That's why I don't like bringing you with me. How will you see the train today? We'll have to sit in the hot sun till late afternoon. We must be off, Khoka. We'll stop by on our way home, how about that?'

Apu had no option but to follow his father, his eyes dim with tears.

They reached their destination after dark. Lakkhan Mahajan, a disciple of his father's, was a prosperous farmer. He greeted them with great courtesy and made arrangements for them to be put up in a big thatched room.

Early next morning, Lakkhan Mahajan's younger brother's wife had gone to bathe in the pond. Just as she was about to step into the water, her eyes fell on a curious sight in the little garden surrounding the pond—a boy was pacing up and down the banana grove with a cane in his hand. He was spouting poetry, muttering away to himself like a mad creature. She laid down her waterpot and came towards him. 'To whose house have you come visiting, little fellow?' she wanted to know.

Apu reserved all his tantrums for his mother. Outside his home he was terribly shy. Addressed by the young woman, he thought at first that he would make a run for it. But then thinking better of it he merely said shyly, 'To their house . . . over there!'

'Oh, you mean my elder brother-in-law's house? Are you his guru's son then?'

The young woman took him home with her. They lived in a different house, separated from the main one of Lakkhan Mahajan's by the bathing pond which lay in between.

Apu soon lost his shyness in the young woman's company.

He observed the interior of their house with a great deal of interest. My, what a lot of things they had inside! They had nothing like this in their own home. They must be really very rich people, he thought. A clothes-stand decorated with shells, colourful pot-holders of rope hanging from the ceiling, birds made of wool, dolls of porcelain and of clay, trees carved of the white pith of shola and a whole heap of other delightful things. A couple of these objects he picked up timidly and examined, running his fingers over them. The young wife, who had been observing Apu, was moved by his innocence. His face had the open and tender expression of a five year old. She had never seen such innocent eyes, such a fine complexion and such delicate features. His pure eyes seemed to have been painted with the finest of strokes. Her heart welled up with affection for the unknown boy.

Meanwhile Apu had settled down amongst all the playthings and was chattering away, especially about the railroad that he had just seen yesterday. A little later the young wife cooked him some delicious mohanbhog, a whole bowl full of it, so rich with ghee that it streaked his fingers when he began eating. Apu just had a morsel and was dumbfounded at the taste, it was so utterly delicious—he had never eaten anything like it. And why did this mohanbhog have raisins in it? When he pestered his mother to make him some mohanbhog she would do so quite happily. She fried the coarse flour of wheat first and then it was boiled in water with tiny lumps of jaggery. It looked much like a poultice when it was served to him on a special plate of bell-metal that she kept for these occasions. Until now, Apu had relished the mohanbhog made by his mother as a special treat; today he realized that there was a world of difference between his mother's mohanbhog and the treat he was now having. Instinctively, he felt very protective of his mother and was filled with compassion for her. Perhaps she did not know that this was how mohanbhog should be cooked. He began to have a dim notion that his mother was poor, that they were poor people and so they couldn't afford to eat the kind of food that other people did.

A few days later Apu was invited to a meal by the next-door Brahmin family. In the afternoon a girl came over to fetch him. She had laid out a low seat in their veranda, sprinkled water and made all the arrangements for his meal. The girl was called Amala. She had a very rosy complexion, big eyes and was quite nice looking. She would have been about the same age as his sister. Amala's mother sat beside Apu throughout the meal, serving him all sorts of delicacies, the meal culminating in a delicious dessert of chandrapuli which she had made herself. After the meal, Amala escorted him back to Lakkhan Mahajan's home.

Later that afternoon, while Apu was having a marvellous time playing with the other boys, his toe got caught between two strips of bamboo of a newly made fence. The strips were still raw and sharp; his toe was badly lacerated and the cut bled freely. If Amala hadn't come running and taken his toe out carefully from between the fencing, he might have lost it. Apu was unable to walk: Amala picked him up and carried him home like a child. She crushed the leaves of the pathurkuchi herb which grew by their paddy stack, pounded it to a paste and bandaged the cut with it. Afraid of a scolding from his father, Apu kept quiet about the accident.

Amala took him home with her. She opened a huge almirah and took out a big porcelain European doll, a wax bird, a tree made of shola and all sorts of astonishing toys. They had been bought, she said, from the famous annual fair at Kaliganj. Apu was taken by the many kinds of toys he had never seen before. There was a rubber monkey which blinked its eyes at you whenever you happened to look at it. And a doll that would flail its arms like an epileptic and start banging on a pair of cymbals if you pressed its tummy. Most amazing of all was a tin horse: you had to wind it—like Ranudi's uncle wound up the clock in their corridor—and it would trot across the entire length of the floor. It went ever so far, just as if it was a real horse. Apu was mesmerized by the horse. He picked it up to look at it closely and asked Amala a heap of questions: What a nice horse, where did you buy it? How much did it cost? Then Amala showed him a little casket for holding sindur. But instead of the vermilion powder, was that a reddish strip of foil gleaming inside?

'Is that coloured foil?' he asked Amala.

'Not coloured foil,' she said. 'Haven't you ever seen a gold leaf?'

Apu had never seen any. But how could gold be so red, he wondered, as he picked it up and turned it over in his hand. While he was being taken back by Amala he reflected, Didi doesn't have any of these toys; she spends all her time collecting bonduc nuts to play and roda seeds to spin with . . . and she gets beaten up because she steals dolls from other girls. Apu had not realized till now what a glorious wealth of toys a girl of his sister's age could have. It was the first time that he had an occasion for comparison and it filled him with deep compassion for his sister. If he had the money he would certainly buy her a clockwork horse and a rubber monkey that would blink at you from whichever direction you happened to look at it.

The young wife who had befriended him on that first day owned a pack of cards. Not exactly a pack; it was made up of all sorts of cards which had been abandoned by their owners. Apu liked fiddling with them every now and then. The women in their village held card sessions at Ranudi's on some afternoons. Apu liked watching them deal . . . Ace, Jack, Queen, King . . . People would sometimes quarrel over the cards, but it was a nice game. He himself didn't know how to play cards; neither did his sister nor his mother. Once in a while his mother would try and join the regular card players but no one wanted her on their side. She doesn't know how to play, they said. If he could get hold of a pack of cards, all three of them— he, his sister and his mother, could get down to playing.

Apu was invited to the young wife's home that evening. When he arrived he was amazed at the variety of food and the elaborate arrangements that had been made for him. Why was there that tiny bowl with salt and slices of lemon in it? His mother always put the salt and lemon slice on one side of his plate. And all those little bowls for every one of the vegetable dishes! What an array of vegetables too! Oh, that gigantic head of a prawn—was that for him? And freshly fried puffy luchis—luchis galore! It was like the very land of dreams that he and his sister conjured up in the blue mists of a fairy-tale world.

A couple of days later Harihar was back home with his son. They had been gone for less than a week, but Sarbojoya was finding the separation from her son almost unbearable. Durga had not enjoyed playing by herself these past few days. A few days before Apu had left on his travels, brother and sister had stopped talking to each other after having fought over boats made of dry pumpkin shells—they'd been making sailboats of them. While Apu was away many such boats had been acquired but Durga had somehow lost interest in sailing them. Why did I fight with him over such a silly thing and why did I box his ears? Let him come back and I'll never fight with him again . . . he can have all the shells, she told herself.

For at least a fortnight after his return, Apu regaled everyone with tales of his travels.

What a range of amazing things he had seen in just the few days they had been gone! The railroad on which real trains ran; custard apples, papayas and cucumbers of clay that looked exactly like real fruit; and a most marvellous doll that flailed its arms about like an epileptic and suddenly started banging on cymbals. And there was Amala, whom he called Amaladi . . . How far they had journeyed, so many ponds and lakes teeming with lotuses, and unknown villages and lonely paths through vast stretches of fields and meadows. He told them about the roadside smithy in an unknown village where his father had taken him for a drink of water. Those kind folks had taken him indoors and had treated him to a meal of milk with parched rice and bits of sugar rounds. He had so many such tales to tell that he didn't know which to choose from. But what thrilled his sister the most was his story of the railroad. She kept asking him, 'How big are the rails, Apu? And was the wire hanging overhead the whole way? Was it very long? And did you get to see a real train?' No-o-o—Apu hadn't actually *seen* a train. This was the only thing he had missed seeing and it was all because of his father. If they had only waited for about five hours, sat quietly by the tracks—they would've seen it for sure. But he had failed to persuade Baba!

It was late in the day and Sarbojoya was entering the house in a hurry. As soon as she stepped in absentmindedly into the yard, something like a thin string struck her chest and immediately snapped; two thin sticks on either side of the yard fell to the ground. It all happened in a flash before she had the time to figure out what was happening.

Apu came home a little later. He stood stock-still as soon as he stepped into the yard. He couldn't believe his eyes. 'What's this! What could've happened? Who has torn my teligiraph wire!'

When he had somewhat absorbed this shattering discovery he looked around and found some footprints in the yard. Something in his heart said, it had to be his mother and nobody else who was the culprit. Had to be Ma!

He found his mother indoors calmly washing jackfruit seeds. Apu ran in and came to a halt, striking a pose much like the hero of a jatra troupe (the way the boy hero Abhimanyu would stand, his body leaning forward) and cried out in his melodious treble, 'Well, Ma! Did I not bring those creeper-ropes from all sorts of wild places with a great deal of trouble?'

Sarbojoya turned to look at him wonderingly and said, 'What did you bring? What are you speaking of?'

'And was it not terribly difficult for me to bring them? And *didn't* I get all scratched and poked by those thorns?'

'What on earth is he going on about like a mad man? What's up?'

'What's up? I hung up those teligiraph wires . . . it was such hard work too—and now they've been simply torn away!'

'Is there a moment when you're not up to your tricks! Always doing something mad! How would I know what had been strung between the stones is your precious teligiraph or feligiraph! I was in a hurry and it must have snapped as I came in. So, what am I supposed to do now?' responded Sarbojoya and she turned back to her work.

Ooh, such cruelty! He did believe at one time that his mother truly loved him, but that was clearly an illusion and had long since disappeared. But never in his wildest dreams had he imagined his mother to be such a cruel, stone-hearted woman. All of yesterday he had scoured the neighbourhood—Uncle Neelmoni's house, the big mango orchard belonging to the Palits, the bamboo grove of Prasanna Guruji; such dense and savage jungles he had braved, all alone, and dragged those thick creepers that hung from the topmost branches—only so that he could play at rails. Everything had been set up so beautifully and now this! It was too much, too unfair.

He was suddenly filled with an intense urge to tell his mother something strong, rude, something deeply wounding. After a bit of thinking he came up with nothing better than, 'I'm not going to eat any rice today . . . so there! I'll never eat any food.' (This was said in higher notes than before.)

'Well, don't then,' replied his mother. 'Like you'll be doing me a special favour by eating rice . . . and you can hardly wait for the rice to cook mostly. If you won't eat, so be it. Let's see who is going to feed you when you are hungry!'

Everything was as before—his mother was still washing the jackfruit seeds, but where was Apu? He had evaporated like camphor! In a flash! Only Durga, who was just entering the house, saw her brother streak past her like a whirlwind. She cried out in surprise, 'Apu, where are you rushing off to? What's happened? Apu, listen—'

'Don't ask me,' exclaimed her mother. 'You kids are always upto some mischief or the other, wearing me down to the bone, the two of you are. He'd strung up something or the other right at the entrance—how would I know—I came in and it snapped. What am I supposed to do? Did I do it on purpose! So the boy is angry, won't eat anything he says. Well, if you don't want to, don't—like you'll be doing me a favour by eating rice . . . earn me a place in heaven or something!'

Durga was obliged to keep peace between mother and son in their passionate quarrels. She went around hunting for her brother, calling out his name, not resting until she discovered him at two in the afternoon. Apu was sitting dejectedly on a fallen mango tree trunk by the Rays' garden, looking quite woebegone.

If a neighbour had happened to drop in at their home later in the day he would have never imagined that this was the same Apu who had renounced hearth and home and had set off for other climes after that spat with his mother. The 'wire' had been strung anew; it now stretched from one end of the yard to another. Apu was taking it all in with great joy and amazement: to think it was exactly like he had seen it, the railroad wire, the real thing! He ran over to Satu's to call him. 'Will you come over to our place, Satuda? I've hung up the teligiraph wire in our yard . . . let's play at trains . . . will you come?'

'Who put up the wire?' Satu wanted to know.

'I did, myself. Didi got me the ropes.'

'Go and play by yourself now,' said Satu. 'I can't come now.'

Apu realized that he was not up to rounding up the bigger boys and getting them to join in the game. Who would listen to him? He tried once more, standing on the edge of their raised veranda, 'Oh come on, Satuda, won't you come?' he asked in a somewhat hopeless voice. 'You and I and Didi—

95

we three can play together.' And then trying to tempt him he added, 'I've picked a heap of pomelo leaves for tickets, you know.' He indicated the hugeness of the pile with a gesture of his hand. 'Will you come?' But Satu didn't want to join him. Apu was terribly shy outside of his home. He came back home without any ado. He was almost ready to weep in his disappointment. He'd tried so hard and still Satuda had not come!

The next morning, he and his sister were playing at shop. They piled up enough bricks to make a big shop and then they set off to put together the goods they were going to sell. Durga kept track of all that grew in the jungle around their house. They made paan out of nona leaves, potatoes of wild yam, fish of radhalata flowers, gourds of the brilliant red telé-kochu, beans of the rangchita, the salt from bits of earth and a whole heap of other stuff besides. By the time their shop had been stocked it was late in the day. 'What will you do for sugar, Didi?' Apu asked.

'You know that mound by the bamboo grove—there's lovely sand to be found there: Ma uses it to roast the rice in . . . we'll get the sand. It's white and shiny, just like sugar.'

They went through the jungle to look for their sugar in the bamboo grove. High up, on the topmost branch of a bonchatka tree, there were some big round fruits. They were a brilliant red, peeping out from behind the thick green tangle of creepers. Apu and Durga were both thrilled at the sight of the rosy red fruits. After much tugging from below they managed to tear off some of the creeper and three of the brilliant red fruits rolled to the ground. They ran to claim their booty. Since there were only three, it was decided that they would be used to attract customers to the shop. The fruits were arranged in such a way as to immediately catch the customer's eye.

Then they got down to the serious business of buying and selling. Durga bought up so many of the paan leaves that she almost depleted the entire stock. The game was really picking up when Apu saw Satu enter their courtyard. He was overwhelmed by this favour and ran to welcome the older boy. 'Satuda! You must come and see what a nice shop we've set up. And look at these fruits . . . Didi and I got them . . . Do you know what they are?'

'Oh, those! They're makal fruits—you can't eat them! We used to have heaps of them in our garden.'

Apu was immensely gratified at Satu's arrival. Satuda rarely came to their place. Besides, Satuda was a sort of leader among the older boys. His presence imparted a certain seriousness to their game, as if it was not just children make-believing.

They were playing with great gusto. Durga said to the shopkeeper, 'Excuse me, can I have two maunds of rice please, really fine grade stuff—it's my doll's engagement ceremony tomorrow, you see, and there'll be many guests.'

'What about us, are we invited?' asked Satu.

'Of course, you are,' said Durga nodding her head in a grown-up manner. 'You are from the bride's side. I'll come in the morning and fetch you all formally. Satuda, will you tell Ranu that she should make some sandal paste for the ceremony? I'll fetch it in the morning.'

Durga had barely finished when Satu made a sudden grab at something from the goods for sale and dashed towards the backdoor. Apu gave him chase, crying out as he did so, 'Didi, he's taken them!' His reed-thin voice was even shriller as he cried out and sped after Satu.

Before Durga could quite understand what had happened, both Apu and Satu had disappeared beyond the door. As she turned back to the shop counter, she realized that all the ripe red makal fruits were missing. Not one was left!

When Durga ran to the door she was in time to see Satu sprinting along the path by the gaub tree and Apu panting after him, about to catch up with him. Satu was several years older than Apu; moreover, he was not slim and girlishly built like Apu but had a sturdy frame. It wasn't expected that Apu would be able to keep up with him. If Apu had almost caught up with Satu it was because Satu was running with stuff he had stolen, while Apu was running for his life, to recover something precious.

Durga saw that Satu suddenly seemed to slow down: now he was stooping. Then he quickly turned back and immediately, Apu stopped as well. The next moment Satu had once more picked up speed and was running beyond the Chalta-tala path before he disappeared from sight.

Meanwhile, Durga had run up to Apu who was crouching

forward and rubbing his eyes. 'What is it, Apu?' she asked anxiously.

Apu was not able to look at her. He kept rubbing his eyes with both his hands and seemed to be in great pain. 'Satuda . . . threw a handful of . . . dust into my eyes, Didi . . . I can't see a thing . . .'

Durga quickly pulled away his hands from his eyes, 'Here, let me see. You needn't go rubbing your eyes like that, dear. Look up.'

But Apu was rubbing his eyes again, 'Didi,' he said in a desperate voice, 'it's hurting, Didi . . . I think he's blinded me, Didi . . .'

'Here, let me see. Don't go on rubbing your eyes so.' She warmed up her sari-end with her breath and put it over his eyes. A little later Apu could open at least one of his eyes and begin looking around him. Durga lifted up his eyelids gently and blew repeatedly on them. 'There, that's better, isn't it? Now you can see again, can't you? You had better go home. I shall go to their place and tell his mother and his grandmother everything. I'll tell Ranu as well—what a horrid boy! You get going; I'll be with you in a minute,' she comforted him.

But having gone as far as the outer door of Ranu's house she was afraid to go any further. She greatly feared Shejo bou. After hesitating for a few moments before their outer door, she turned back to her own home. When she pushed open the front door she found Apu sheltering behind one of the door panels, weeping silently.

Apu was not the sort to cry; he could get angry and sulk or look hurt but he rarely cried. Durga knew that he must have been badly hurt by what had taken place just now. Not only had their precious fruits been snatched away so unexpectedly, he had dust flung into his eyes as well. Durga could never bear to see Apu cry and now she felt as if her heart would break. She went forward to hold his hand and comfort him. 'Don't cry, Apu. Come, I'll give you all my cowrie shells. Are your eyes hurting again? Ohh! You've torn your dhoti, too . . .'

On most days after they had had their afternoon meal, Apu would stay indoors. It was an old room in their dilapidated ancestral home. The room was stuffed with all sorts of things—ancient iron safes, old-fashioned faded cane baskets, a clothes-stand, low wooden seats and bedsteads. There were also many boxes and chests that Apu had never seen being opened. They contained jars and pitchers, but he was ignorant of what else they may have held. Altogether, the room let out a funny smell of old and musty things. He wasn't quite sure exactly what the smell was, but it seemed to remind him of bygone days—of a time when he was not there, but the clothes-stand with the shells was, as was the cane basket that belonged to his grandfather, and so too that big wooden chest. Not far away was a temple dedicated to Goddess Chandi, there—where the golden laburnum trees reared their heads out of the jungle . . . how many children, each one with his or her own name, must have played right there where now it was overgrown with weeds and jungly plants . . . they had turned to shadows and were now gone forever . . . all so long ago!

When he was alone at home and his mother had gone to the ghat, he was seized with a great desire and curiosity to open that ancient cane basket, those boxes and chests and to uncover whatever mysteries they seemed to hold. On the topmost wooden shelf of the crossbeam lay a heap of palm-leaf manuscripts and notebooks in the big box. He had found out from his father that they had belonged to his grandfather, Pandit Ramchand Tarkalankar. How he wished that they were within his reach! He would have brought them down and gone through them. On some days he sat by the window, looking out into the jungle, and read from the tattered copy of Kashiram Das's Mahabharata. He had already learnt to read quite well; he didn't need to wait any more for someone to read out to him. Not only did he read fluently, he understood much of what he read as well. He was sharp in his studies. Sometimes, his father would take him to the Chandi shrine at the Gangulys' where the elders sat around in the evening. His father would hand him a copy of the Ramayana or *Dashu Ray's Panchali* and say, 'Here, my boy, why don't you read this aloud? Let them hear you read.'

The elders were full of praise for the boy. 'That wretched grandson of mine,' Dinu Chatterjee would complain. 'Same age as your boy; must've torn to shreds a couple of primers at least. You wouldn't believe it if I were to tell you, but he can just about recognize the alphabet! Takes after his father I'm sure. As soon as I'm dead and gone, he'll have no choice but to take up a plough and fend for himself.'

Harihar's breast would swell with pride at his son's achievements. 'How could the likes of you do well,' he would muse, 'after all, moneylending is what you've been doing for generations. We may be poor, but we do come from a lineage of pandits. Not for nothing did Baba fill up all those manuscripts . . . he's left us a tradition to inherit—learning that's bound to reveal itself . . .'

A few yards from their window was the boundary wall and a huge jungle of weeds and bushes started right where the wall stood. From the window you could only see a green sea—the tops of ghetu and sheora trees with all sorts of creepers winding around them, copses of ancient bamboos bending and swooping to touch the ground, and wild chalta trees in whose shadow the wagtail danced on the black soil below.

Under the bigger trees grew a maze of turmeric, wild taro, bitter corm—a green jungle jostling for space, desperately searching out the sun. The jungle continued right up to the field by the old indigo bungalow and beyond, along the river. To Apu, this stretch of jungle seemed immense, unending. He had often roamed the jungle with his sister but had never quite seen where it actually ended. You picked your way through heaps of wild chalta fruits strewn everywhere, beneath tittiraj trees from which hung thick coils of gulancha creepers. The narrow path ended in a mango orchard and then it trailed off this way and that through thorny bushes and forbidding thickets of wild kalmi and pandanus bushes with their serrated edges, taking you where sponge gourd creepers swayed resplendently in mid air, and the mossy branches of ancient shirish trees were festooned with orchids.

Somewhere in this jungle lay an old silted-up pond and, somewhere by the pond, a ruined temple. Just as Panchananda Thakur was now the presiding deity of the village, so had this temple been dedicated to Vishaalakshi Devi, sometime in the past. She had been consecrated as the patron goddess of the village and the temple established by the Majumdar family. But once, after they had been blessed with success in some affair, they had performed a human sacrifice to her. Displeased by this act, the Devi had appeared in a dream and announced that henceforth she would have nothing to do with the village temple. She forsook the temple and never came back.

It had happened a long time ago. There was none alive today who had seen worship being offered to Vishaalakshi. The temple lay in ruins, the pond in front of the temple had long since dried up and the jungle had silently taken over. Of the Majumdar family no descendant was left to light the ritual evening lamp to the gods.

Only once—and that too many years ago—Swarup Chakravarty was returning home from an invitation at a neighbouring village. When he had come down to the river ghat he saw a beautiful sixteen-year-old girl. The place was far from human habitation, it was already dark and there was not a soul in sight. Swarup Chakravarty was completely taken aback at finding a beautiful young girl all alone in that lonely forest. But before he could say anything, the girl said in a melodious but proud voice, 'I am Vishaalakshi Devi, I am of this village. The village is soon going to face a cholera epidemic. Tell the villagers that they should sacrifice 108 pumpkins on the fourteenth night of the lunar month and perform a puja to Goddess Kali.' Barely had these words been uttered when, right before the eyes of the spellbound Swarup Chakravarty, the girl seemed to dissolve in the misty winter evening. And true to her words, a few days later the village was struck by a terrible epidemic.

Apu had heard these stories ever so often. Whenever he stood by the window he would think of Vishaalakshi Devi. Might it not be possible for *him* to have a vision of Vishaalakshi Devi? Perhaps he would be plucking gulancha creepers along the jungle path . . . when suddenly, an extraordinarily beautiful girl wearing a red-bordered sari, necklace and bangles glinting upon her neck and hands like Goddess Durga, would appear . . .

'Who are you?' she would ask him.

'I am Apu.'

'You are such a good boy; what is the boon you desire?'

On some afternoons Apu would lie down on the bed. A sudden breeze would bring in bitter-sweet wafts of fragrance from the jungle outside. A river gull would send out its long drawn-out cry as it glided over a banyan tree. He never quite knew when he would have fallen asleep. When he would wake up the day would be gone. Outside the window shadows would have encircled the jungle, the tips of the bamboo clusters glowing red in the fading light. Enchanting wondrous evenings. Beside the thickly shadowed trees is their little playroom. The wire made of gulancha creepers is strung across the yard, by the door woven of date-palm branches. Cool flavours drift in from the wood, the pomelo tree in the ruins of their uncle's place is lit with rosy tints, and the tero bird with its glinting nut-coloured wings flits from bush to bush. The smell of fresh earth fills his being and his boyish heart overflows with joy. Can he ever express this joy to anyone?

13

Vulture eggs

Apu had come to where the fisherfolk lived hoping to play at cowries with the boys there. After he had unsuccessfully done the rounds of all the usual spots in the area his eyes lit up when he finally came across a group under the tamarind tree near Baburam Padui's house. An exciting game was on under the tree. Most of the players were fisherboys; Potu, who was a couple of years younger than him, was the only one other Brahmin boy. Apu didn't know him very well for he lived at a distance from them. Apu remembered that the first day he was taken to Prasanna Guruji's school it was this boy who had been quietly chewing on the palm leaf that he was meant to write on.

'How many cowries do you have?' Apu asked.

'I've brought seventeen with me,' said Potu, taking out his little pouch of cowries. 'Seven of them are special golden ones; if I lose these I'll fetch some more.' Then holding up his pouch with a smile he asked Apu, 'What do you think of this? It holds about twenty cowries!' The pouch was made of interwoven coloured skeins of thread and was a dear possession of his.

The game began. At first Potu kept losing but gradually, he started to win. Potu had discovered only a few days ago that he had become quite skilled in the game, and now he was seized by dreams of conquest. That is why he had come so far away from home. Following the rules of the game, he would take aim with a big cowrie and hit his target, which would inevitably come out spinning from inside the marked-out 'house' and Potu would beam with joy at his victory. Picking up the cowries he had won he savoured the sight of his ever swelling pouch, glancing every now and then during the game to see if it was quite full.

A few of the fisherboys now put their heads together and held a muttered discussion. 'Master,' said one of them to Potu, 'you will have to go back a few paces and hit the target: you are too good a shot.'

'Why should I do that?' countered Potu. 'As though it's my fault that I've a good aim. Why don't you win some cowries? It's not like I've ordered you not to win.' He looked up to find the fisherboys huddled together. 'I've never won so many cowries before,' he thought. 'I shan't play any more today . . . won't be able to take these back home if I do. It's too much—that extra distance they want . . . I'll lose them all.' Abruptly he picked up his pouch and said, 'I won't play

107

from a further distance; I'm going home.' But when he saw the fisherboys and their cruel gaze on him, unconsciously his hand tightened over his pouch.

'That's not on, Master,' said one coming up to him. 'You think you'll run off after you've won all our cowries.' And he made a sudden lunge at the hand in which Potu held his pouch. Potu tried to free his hand but he was no match for the older boy in strength. 'What are you doing! Let go of my hand!' he cried out. Someone shoved him from behind. He fell on the ground but held on still to his pouch. He realized that it was the pouch they were after. He tried desperately to slide the pouch under his stomach but he was a mere boy and not as strong as they were, the fisherboys were older and muscular: how long could he hold out against them? The pouch was thrown aside in the scuffle and his precious cowries tumbled out and scattered all over the place.

At first, Apu was not too unhappy about Potu's plight, for he too had lost many of his cowries to the younger boy. But when he saw Potu falling down and all the boys beating him as he lay there helplessly, he was deeply affected. He pushed his way through the crowd, 'He's just a little boy—why are you all ganging up against him? Let go of him, let go!' He was leaning forward to help Potu up but someone gave him such a blow from behind that for a while he was stunned. And then, he too fell to the ground in the melée.

Apu could not talk about this incident; he didn't mention it to anyone, not even to his sister.

That afternoon, when his father was away, he shut the door and secretly opened the old chest of books. Eagerly, he leafed through the books, looking at the pictures and hunting for interesting stories. On the title pages of one of the books he read *Sarbadarshan Sangraha*, or *Compendium of All Philosophies*. He hadn't a clue as to what the title meant or what the contents might be. The bound cover of old marbled paper was damaged in many places. As soon as he opened the book a row of silverfish darted out from beneath the faded marbled cover page and dashed off in every direction. Apu brought the book close to his nose and took a deep breath, inhaling the old and musty smell. He loved the smell given off by the thick reddish pages: somehow, he associated it with his father. These old books fascinated him. He put away the other books, but this one he hid under his pillow. It was while he was secretly going through the book that he came upon an astonishing bit of information, something that made him shiver in excitement. True, if he had simply *heard* of it somewhere he too would have been suspicious, but here it was in print—right inside a book—and he was reading it. The author, in enumerating the many properties of mercurium had written: If mercurium is put inside vulture's eggs and those eggs sunned for a few days, and if they are then placed inside one's mouth, one can propel oneself in the atmosphere, i.e. fly!

Apu could not believe his own eyes. He read the passage once again and then over and over. He stuffed the book deep inside his own box with the broken lid and went outdoors to ponder over this incredible bit of information.

'Didi,' he asked his sister, 'do you know where vultures nest?' But his sister didn't know. He asked every single boy he knew—Satu, Nipu, Kinu, Potol, Neda . . . Someone said, not hereabouts, far away in the North Field on the top of very tall trees . . .

'Where do you go off wandering every day in the heat of the afternoon?' his mother scolded. Apu went indoors, pretending to sleep. Instead, he leafed through the book once more. Astonishing! But how did no one else know that there was such an easy way to fly? Was it because other people did not have this particular book in their homes: only his father owned such a book; or perhaps, others had missed reading this section—only he had chanced to read the passage in all this time? He buried his face in the book and once more inhaled that familiar musty scent. He had full faith in the contents. As for 'mercurium', he knew that meant quicksilver: he wasn't worried about that. Mirrors have a backing of quicksilver; and they had a broken mirror at home. It wouldn't be a problem getting hold of *that*; but how was he going to lay his hands on vulture eggs?

After much enquiry there was a ray of hope. Cowherds tethered their cows to the big jackfruit tree by Hiru the barber's house when they went to collect their wages of oil and tobacco from other householders. Apu sought out one of the boys, 'You roam all over the place grazing your cattle:

have you ever spotted a vulture's nest? If you can fetch me some vulture eggs I'll give you two paise.'

A few days later, the cowherd was at their outer door calling out for Apu. He took out two little black eggs from a pouch strung on his waist. 'Here, I've got you the eggs, Master,' he said to Apu.

Apu quickly put out his hand, 'Let's see.' He turned over the eggs in his hands delightedly. 'Vulture eggs! You're sure, aren't you?'

The boy gave Apu a pile of proofs maintaining that indeed they were vulture eggs. He claimed that he had risked his life to climb up to the topmost branch of a very tall tree; he even gave particulars of the exact location in which the tree was to be found. But he wouldn't settle for less than two annas for the eggs.

Apu was in despair at the price put on the eggs. 'I'll give you the two paise and my cowries besides,' he tried to bargain. 'I'll give them all to you—a whole tin box full of cowries. Such big golden ones I've got: want to see them? Shall I show them to you?'

The cowherd appeared to be infinitely more worldly wise than Apu. He was unwilling to accept anything but cash. Finally, after a lot of haggling the deal was struck at four paise. Apu begged and begged his sister till she gave him two paise and then at long last, when the cowherd had been given his four paise and some cowries as well, he was allowed to lay hands on the eggs. The cowries he had just handed over were as dear as life to Apu. At no other time would he have parted with them for love or money, not even for half a kingdom and a princess. But what was a game of cowries to the joys of flying in the air!

As soon as the eggs were in his hand he felt his heart expanding and soaring like a balloon. Then, the faintest shadow of a doubt passed through his mind. At dusk he sat down on the sawn-off trunk of the mango tree at Neda's house and began worrying: Would he really be able to fly? And where should he fly to? To his uncle? Or towards where his father had gone? To the other side of the river? Like a mynah or a starling he would fly into the sky far away where the stars were even now beginning to twinkle . . .

The next day or perhaps a few days later, just before dusk, Durga was hunting for rags to make wicks for the lamps. While she was groping among the bundle of rags on the high shelf with its burden of unused pots, pans and other rubbish, something hit against the vessels and rolled down on to the floor. It was quite dark inside the room; she couldn't see clearly. Durga picked up whatever was on the floor and went outside for a good look. Goodness! Eggs! Where could they have come from? Oh! They're all smashed up. 'Ma, do come see these eggs . . . what bird would've laid its eggs here?'

It would be discreet to draw the curtain on what happened next. Apu didn't touch a morsel of food the entire day. There were tears, tantrums, a regular hullabaloo.

'Whatever shall I do with the boy!' his mother was saying

to her friends at the riverside. 'Have you ever heard of such a thing! Humans can fly if they have vulture eggs in their mouth! He caught hold of the cowherd who works for our neighbour and the fellow got him a pair of crow eggs or something like that and told him—here's your vulture eggs, and I believe he actually paid *four* whole paise for those eggs! That boy is such an innocent fool—it really makes me anxious. What am I to do with him . . .'

How was Sarbojoya to know? Not everyone had gone through the *Compendium of All Philosophies*, nor was everyone aware of the superior properties of mercurium. If they had, they would all have been flying in the skies.

14

Champa blossoms

For a long time now, Apu had been great friends with old Narottam Das Babaji of the village. Fair-complexioned Narottam, who lived in a simple one-room thatched hut, was always joyous, radiating happiness in his very being. He didn't care much for anything that would disturb his solitude. He was happy in his own company, away from any kind of bustle. From the time that Apu was a mere child Harihar had been taking his son to Narottam Das and the two had always hit it off. As he grew older, Apu would often turn up at the old man's house and call out, 'Gran'pa, are you home?' The old man would hurry out from his hut and lay out a palm-leaf mat on the little terrace for the boy. 'Come, come little brother, do come and take a seat.'

Elsewhere, you could hardly get the shy Apu to speak a

word, but he spoke freely with the simple old man as if he was a playmate of his own age. Narottam Das had no family and lived by himself. A young Vaishnav girl, of the same community, came in twice a day to do the housework and to look in on him. Apu sometimes whiled away a whole afternoon engrossed in chatting with him. He knew that the Babaji was much older than his father. But this very fact somehow made Apu feel that the older man was a close companion of his. When he came to visit him, he shed his fears and his shyness without quite knowing how. He laughed heartily as they swapped stories and spoke of things that he would have hesitated to express elsewhere for fear of being snubbed or being rebuked by elders as being too 'precocious'.

For his part, Narottam Das believed that Apu was just as the divine Gaurango himself must have been as a boy. 'My beloved Gaur must have been as enchanting and as innocent as you—he too must have had the same dreamy, other-worldly expression in his beautiful eyes,' he would say.

Apu would have found such sentiments embarrassing in any other context, but here, he merely laughed and demanded, 'In that case, Gran'pa, won't you show me the pictures in that big book you have?' The elder man would bring out his copy of the sacred Vaishnav text, *Prembhakti Chandrika*. It was one of his most favourite books of the Vaishnav canon and it never failed to move him whenever he read it in solitude. The book had only two illustrations: after they had both admired the pictures, the elder said,

'When I die, my little brother, I shall leave the book for you, for I know that you will truly care for it.'

Apu intuitively grasped that the unpretentious mode of life that he experienced on these visits carried the very breath of a spiritual freedom. It was as intimate and joyous as the touch of fresh earth, the special delight he had in the many birds, plants and trees that he discovered afresh, every day. That was why he was drawn to this Gran'pa of his and longed to visit him.

On his way home from these visits he always picked up an armful of the muchukundu champa blossoms that had fallen from the tree in Narottam Das's courtyard. Apu laid the blossoms tenderly on his bed. As soon as the evening lamp was lit, he had to sit down to study, in obedience to his father's wishes. He was required to study for an hour at the most, but to Apu it seemed like hours passed and it was almost night time before he was done. Then came the evening meal, and finally, it was time to go to bed. Memories of the games he had been playing and the little pleasures of the day enveloped his tired body, and lying down on his stomach, he plunged his face into the heap of champa flowers, taking in their fragrance with every breath . . .

15

A feast

'What do you say to a picnic, Apu? We'll cook outdoors, huh?' Durga asked her brother one day. It was to be a secret.

Towards the end of the year all the neighbours would go past their house to the field on the outskirts of the village to cook a meal in the woods. It was part of the seasonal observances for a ritual dedicated to the Goddess Kuluichandi. Their mother too would join this group of women, but nowadays she did not take Apu along with her. Each woman had to carry her own ingredients for the cookout, but *they* never seemed to have all that was needed. The other women would take out all the nice things they had brought from their home—milk, ghee, potatoes and fine quality rice and pulses. Sarbojoya would have brought a handful of coarse grained rice, a boiled paste of split-peas and a couple of brinjals. Right next to her, the children from

Bhubon Mukherjee's would be sitting down to a hearty meal of milk, rice and bananas flavoured with freshly made palm jaggery. Sarbojoya would think of her own children and feel sad. She knew how fond her Apu was of eating this mix of milk, banana and rice sweetened with fragrant jaggery.

Now Durga was using a machete to clean out a patch of the jungle that grew on the ruins of Neelmoni Ray's house. She called out to her brother, 'Apu, will you come and stand watch here to see if Ma's coming past the tamarind tree? I'll be back right away with some rice and dal.'

Quickly she ladled out two spoonfuls of oil into the half-shell of a coconut. She brought out the other ingredients and transferred them to Apu, 'Quick, run and put them down beside our cooking spot. Don't let the cows get at them.' With the jungle surrounding them, they were hidden from all eyes. The rice she put to boil in a little clay pot that looked like a child's plaything. 'Apu, look, I've got such big potato yams . . . found them, you know, by that palm near Putu's—they were growing on a climber. We'll boil them with the rice!'

Apu scurried around with great enthusiasm collecting dry wood and other odds and ends by way of fuel. This was their very first picnic in the woods. He couldn't believe that they would actually be cooking real rice and real vegetables . . . Or was it going to be like all the other times when they had played at cooking . . . with rice made of dust and potato chips of broken bits of tiles and jackfruit leaves for flaky luchis?

What a glorious day it was! And the spot they had chosen was just right. The first day of spring saw shiny new leaves sprouting on the bushes; a profusion of fragrant ghetu flowers made the ruins of Neelmoni Ray's house radiant with colour and life. Much of the pomelo blossoms had fallen off in the mist and wind of the last few days, but one could still see thick clusters of white flowers on top of the tree.

While they were halfway through their adventure a voice was heard in their courtyard. 'Sounds like Bini's,' said Durga. 'Why don't you go and fetch her, Apu?'

A few minutes later, a dark girl about Durga's age turned up behind Apu. She gave a shy little laugh and asked in a slightly awed voice, 'What are you doing, Dugga didi?'

'Come Bini, sit right here,' said Durga warmly. 'We're having a cookout!'

Bini, a plain-looking tall girl, was the daughter of Kalinath Chakravarti who lived on the other side of the village. She had on a none-too-clean sari and a few glass bangles by way of ornaments on her arms. The Chakravarti family weren't well off and lived practically in a corner of the village. They were never invited on social occasions because they didn't qualify as proper Brahmins, as Kalinath acted as a priest for the lower castes.

Bini happily began running errands for Durga, as though in the course of her rounds of the village she had stumbled on something very precious.

'Bini!' called out Durga. 'Can you get us a couple of more pieces of driftwood—the fire doesn't seem to be doing well.'

Bini promptly ran off and came back a little later with a huge pile of dry twigs. 'Will this be enough, Dugga didi, or shall I get some more?'

When Durga said to her brother, 'Bini's come: she must eat with us too; Apu, go and get some more rice—quick!', Bini's face glowed with delight. She went off to fetch water and then asked Durga enthusiastically, 'And what have you been cooking, Dugga didi?' Durga took off the pot of rice from the fire and fried the brinjal pieces in the little oil they had. She stared in astonishment at her own handiwork: 'Apu, do you see, it's taking on the same colour as Ma's brinjals when she fries them! It's *'xactly* like when Ma fries brinjal, isn't that so?'

Apu too found this phenomenon nothing short of magical. He still couldn't believe that their cookout would produce real rice and real brinjal fries.

The three sat down to eat with great jubilation. The banana-leaf plates were ready. The menu was rice and fried brinjal. As Apu was about to have his first mouthful, Durga asked eagerly, 'How is the fried brinjal?'

'It's nice,' said Apu after a hasty mouthful. 'Looks like it needs some salt, though . . .'

By an oversight, they had completely dispensed with salt in their cooking. Nevertheless, they proceeded to eat with great pleasure the rice with the slightly bland potato yams and the half-burnt pieces of fried brinjal—their menu for the picnic. This was Durga's very first attempt at cooking and the first time that they were having a meal of real rice and real vegetables cooked outdoors. Sitting by a heap of dry leaves and plants beside the fallen fronds of the date-palm, Durga was laughing happily and smiling at Apu while they ate. In her joy she seemed ready to choke on the ball of rice that she was eating.

'Dugga didi, is there some oil?' Bini stopped eating to ask timidly. 'I would've mixed it with the rice and the potato yam . . .'

'Apu, run and get us some oil,' ordered Durga.

'Didi, what are you going to tell Ma?' asked Apu. 'Will you have rice for dinner once more?'

'What! As though one could ever tell Ma. As for dinner, you're sure to be hungry by evening.'

If Bini wanted some drinking water from anyone in the neighbourhood, because of her family's low status, she was offered it in a metal vessel and then too, she was obliged to scour it and wash it well after she had used it. Bini hesitated for a bit before she plucked up enough courage to point to Apu's glass and ask, 'Will you pour some water into my mouth, Apu? I'm very thirsty.'

'Why don't you take it?' said Apu. 'Take it yourself and drink from it.'

Bini still hesitated, afraid.

'Go on, take it, Bini,' urged Durga. 'Take the glass and have a drink of water.'

'No point throwing away the cooking pot,' said Durga after the meal was over. 'We'll cook out in the woods again, right?

Let me hang it up on the branch of that tree with berries, okay?'

'Huh! As if it'll stay there! Mato's Ma comes this way to gather kindling—she's sure to take it away if she spots it, Didi,' Apu warned her.

Durga carefully stowed the pot away in a hole in the crumbling wall.

16

The little golden casket

A few days later . . .

Ranu's elder sister had just been married off and Bhubon Mukherjee's place was still full of relatives who had come for the wedding. Durga had made friends with a little girl called Tuni from among the many children who had come along with their parents for the festivities.

A little before dusk that day, Shejo bou heard Tuni's mother searching for something in the next room. 'What is it, Hashi? What's the matter?' she asked, hurrying towards her.

Tuni's mother, Hashi, was rummaging through the beds—lifting up pillows and mattresses, obviously looking for something. 'I put my little golden casket—where I keep the sindur—right here, next to the bed, some time ago. Then the little one began crying so I went to hush him and didn't think to put it away, but I can't seem to find it anywhere now. Where could it have gone?'

'You don't say so! Are you sure you didn't take it to the next room with you?'

'No, Didi. I kept it right here ... I remember that clearly; right here.'

Both spent some more time hunting for the casket but there was no sign of it. Shejo bou began investigating the whereabouts and movements of various people. She found out that the children of this house had been playing in the passage, and had all left together when they had been called for lunch earlier in the day. All, excepting for the one outsider who had stayed behind—Durga.

Shejo bou's youngest daughter, Tepi, now whispered into her mother's ear, 'You know, Ma, when we were going away for lunch I saw Dugga didi slip out by the backdoor ... she's come back only now!'

Shejo bou held a whispered consultation with some of the assembled relatives and turned to address Durga roughly, 'Give me back the casket, Durga! Tell me, where have you hidden it? Take it out right now, I say, otherwise—'

Durga's face had puckered up in fear. Her mouth dried up at the very sight of Shejo bou and her throat muscles refused to work. She mumbled something but it was barely audible.

Tuni's mother had been silent all this while. She had been taken aback at everyone pouncing on a girl who came from a good family, accusing her of theft. Moreover, she had been seeing something of Durga for the last few days and she had rather liked her: was it possible that the girl would steal?

She spoke up, 'Didi, I don't think she took the casket . . . why would she do—'

She was cut short by Shejo bou. 'You stay out of this! What do you know of her or as to whether she'd have stolen it or not? I know her very well.'

Someone said to Durga, 'Well, if you've taken it, why don't you bring it back or at least tell us where it is? And that's an end to the matter. Come on dearie, give it back. Why lie—'

Durga was in a terrible state. She was feeling weak and her knees were trembling. She leaned against the wall and only said, 'I wouldn't know, Auntie, I'm telling you the truth.'

'You think I'm going to believe her if she says she hasn't taken it!' cried Shejo bou. 'She's the one: I can make out from the way she's behaving. All right, I'm asking you nice and soft: bring it back from wherever you've hidden it and nothing will be said. Won't say a word more if you give back the stuff. All I want is my sindur casket.'

The above-mentioned relative remarked at this point, 'Never knew a gentleman's daughter to steal . . . does she live hereabouts?'

'So, kind words won't do you any good, huh?' said Shejo bou to Durga. 'I'll show you what's what, I'll teach you a lesson. Do you think you're going to pick up and run off with things from *my* house? Do you think you can get away with anything! I'll show you—'

She held Durga by her hand and dragged her to the middle of the passage. 'Tell me, Dugga, where have you kept it? You won't! No, you "don't know" . . . you're a baby . . . you don't know nothing . . . huh! Out with it, or I'll knock out every tooth of yours with a pestle. I'll grind your teeth to powder. Speak, say something, out with it!'

Tuni's mother had run forward to free Durga from Shejo bou's grasp.

'Hold on,' someone said to her, 'can't you see she is the culprit? A beating is the only dose for a thief. Give it back I say, and that's that. Why keep lying—'

Durga's head was ringing. She looked around helplessly and struggled to push her dry tongue to form some words, 'Auntie, I don't know . . . when they all left . . . I too . . .' and keeping her terror-stricken gaze on Shejo bou, she inched her way with her back to the wall.

The crowd of people sought to reason with her for some time. But Durga had only one phrase to say, that she didn't know.

'Hardened critter!' commented one.

'Auntie, she won't even let the mangoes in our garden fall to the ground: picks them off every time,' added Tepi for good measure.

This last comment must have struck a raw wound in Shejo bou. Suddenly she let out a ferocious yell, 'You rascally girl! You thieving . . . of a thief! You won't give us back our own things! I'll see if you don't—' and she fell on Durga with her might. 'Tell me, tell me where have you hidden it,' she cried out in harsh tones, banging Durga's head against the wall furiously. 'Tell me right away. Out with it now!'

Tuni's mother ran up and held Shejo bou by her arm. 'Didi! Didi! What are you doing! Let my casket be; why should you hit her in that way! Let her go. Enough is enough! For shame.'

Tuni had burst into tears at the beating.

'Oh, she's bleeding!' exclaimed the distant relative.

No one had noticed so far that Durga was bleeding profusely from her nose. The sari around her breast had turned red with the blood.

'Tepi, go and fetch some water quick,' ordered Tuni's mother, 'there's a bucket on the veranda.'

The noise and the hullabaloo brought out the daughters and daughters-in-law of the neighbouring household. Ranu's mother had gone over to the smith family next door after lunch for a little chat; she too hurried back.

Durga was quite dizzy from the blows and slaps she had got. She looked up once in a dazed fashion, staring helplessly at someone or something in the crowd.

When the water was brought Ranu's mother washed her eyes and face and made her sit and rest. She was so disoriented she allowed herself to be sat down like she was spellbound. 'You shouldn't have hit her like that, Didi,' Ranu's mother upbraided her sister-in-law. 'A thin creature like her, poor thing. For shame!'

'You've not seen through her yet! A beating is the only medicine for a thief, let me tell you. There's hardly been any beating yet ... we've still not got back our casket. You think I'll let her go just like that? Let Hari Ray hang me or put me on the stake if he wants to—'

'That's quite enough, Didi! Let her recover a bit. After all the ruckus you've created . . .' said Ranu's mother.

'I'd never have mentioned the sindur casket had I known what it would lead to. I don't want my casket. Didi, let her go,' said Tuni's mother.

It is hard to say whether Shejo bou would have yielded up her prey so easily, but popular opinion was now turning against her. She had no choice but to let the accused go.

Ranu's mother held Durga by the hand and walked her to their outer door. 'What a day it has turned out for you! Now, walk home slowly . . . Tepi! Hold open the backdoor, will you?'

17

'Lost my nose-ring dear'

It was time for the annual Charak festival, celebrated by the village as a community event. One of the organizers was Baidyanath Mazumdar who went around with a subscription book hoping to get funds from every householder.

'I must say Uncle,' said Harihar, 'it's not quite fair to expect a rupee each this time. Do I have the means to pay a whole rupee?'

'It's different this time—it's Neelmoni Hazra's troupe that we're getting this year! No one's ever seen anything like them in these parts.'

As a prelude to Charak puja the village boys, dressed as sannyasis, went door to door singing gajon songs, in praise of Shiva. Apu and Durga almost gave up eating and sleeping for these twelve days and wandered all over the village in the tracks of the boy sannyasis who sang and danced the gajon. The other villagers rewarded the players with old clothes, gifts of uncooked food arranged in a tray, money, waterpots, but their family could not afford to give anything except for a handful of rice. That was why this group of players never came to their home.

After the twelve days of gajon singing and dancing, on the eve of Charak, Neel puja was performed in honour of Shiva. On this day the boy sannyasis performed the ritual of 'leaping into the thorns' after first beating and flattening out the sharp and thorny parts of a small date-palm. Durga came home with the news that the sannyasis had already chosen a new tree by the river for this year. Apu and Durga turned up at the new location along with a huge gaggle of children. After the ritual dancing was over the crowd moved to take a round of the field where the Charak would take place. The ritual space for the Neel puja had been encircled with branches of the date-palm and the field had been cleared of sheora trees and other wild plants. There, Apu and Durga met up with the girls from Bhubon Mukherjee's household—Ranu, Puti and Tunu. These girls had nothing of the freedom that Durga enjoyed. Durga wandered at will practically anywhere she chose to, while they were kept under strict watch at home. It had taken a great deal of coaxing and cajoling to be allowed to come up to the Charak Field, escorted by their brother, Neelu.

'The sannyasis will be going to the cremation ground tonight for the wake,' began Tunu.

'As if we don't know!' retorted Ranu. 'One of them will be the corpse and the others will tie him up and take him to the cremation ground by the chhatim tree. There they'll bring him back to life again. And then they'll get a skull and then they'll come this way saying all those rhymes—you know there are spells for all this stuff they do.'

'I know the rhyme—want to hear it?' said Durga. And she rattled off:

From the heavens came the chariot
Down to khetu-tala:
Twenty-four crores, arrow and spear,
Along with Shiva they all appear.
The dead from Satya-yuga,
And the soil from Aul-yuga.
Say Shiva Shiva brother dear;
Strike the drums wihout fear!

'Neeluda,' she added with a smile, 'have you seen what a wonderful image they've made of the boy Krishna? I had a peek at it at Dasu potter's. You've seen it, Ranu?'

'Ranudi, will it be a real skull, of a dead man?' Puti wanted to know more about the sannyasis.

''Course, it will! If you come here really late at night, you'll get to see it.'

'Let's go home. It's not the sort of night that you'd

want to be out of doors. Come on Apu, Dugga, come back with us.'

'Why isn't it *that* sort of night?' asked Apu. 'What is going to happen tonight, Ranudi?'

'Shhh, shouldn't even speak of such things ... now come back with us.'

Durga left with the other children, but Apu stayed on. Clouds suddenly appeared and darkened the evening sky. Walking back home, Apu found himself alone. All those stories about the burning ground, the wake, the skulls, now began to play on his mind and he gradually worked himself up to a state of terror. As he neared the bamboo copse at the crossroads he sensed a peculiar unpleasant smell. He quickened his pace and little later almost ran into Neda's grandmother. Carrying a plate of offerings for Shiva she was on her way to the Charak-tala. At first Apu couldn't recognize her in the dark; then when he did, he asked her, 'Grannie, what's this funny smell that's spreading all—'

'Hush! "They" come out in the evening, don't you know! The smell is because of "them",' replied she.

'Who is "they"?' persisted Apu.

'Who else but "those" that 'company Shiva. Won't do to speak of "them" with the evening upon us. Rama, Rama, Rama, Rama ...' she muttered as an additional protection against the spirits.

Apu shivered. The black evening enveloped them. The sky was full of dark clouds and the bamboo copse was pervaded with the smell of the burning ground . . . Shiva's followers, ghosts and goblins . . . His childish mind was filled with fear and excitement, thrilling at the unknown. 'How shall I go home, Grannie?' he cried out in fear.

'What on earth has kept you outdoors, today of all days!' the old woman scolded him. 'Come along with me now. I'll have to take my plate of offerings to Charak-tala first, then I'll see you home. What a bundle of trouble you are!' she grumbled.

The grass had been cut and the weeds cleared and a huge pavilion erected on the community ground. Any moment now the troupe of jatra players would arrive. There were fresh announcements of their arrival every quarter which invariably ended in disappointment. Slowly, as the evening turned to night, people would say, 'Ah, they're sure to be here by morning,' and when the next day was half gone, they said, 'But they're certain to be here by afternoon.' Apu had but this one thought in his head; he had given up on eating, bathing or sleeping at the usual hours. At night he would be tossing and turning on his bed, unable to sleep properly . . . the jatra players were coming . . . They were going to see jatra performances, jatra . . . jatra . . . jatra . . .

Durga came back with accounts of how the performance space was being decorated with strings of red and blue bunting hanging from the bamboo frames—she had secretly gone to have a peek. Apu found it inconceivable that the very ordinary spot near Panchanan-tala where he and his friends played at cowries every day should have been magically transformed to the performance space for Neelmoni Hazra's famous jatra troupe. He could hardly believe it!

Suddenly, word came that the players were definitely going to be in later that afternoon. The blood shot up to his head. He was absolutely stunned.

From early afternoon onwards, Apu stood watching with the other boys at the crossroads in the potter's colony. Just before dusk he sighted a bullock cart . . . it was still very far away. It was the first of the carts, laden with costumes and what not.

'One . . . two . . . three . . . four . . . five . . . of them!' cried Potu delightedly, counting them one by one with his finger as the carts made a slow appearance. 'Apuda, let's follow them right up to where they're going to be put up; will you come?' Behind the carts came the players on foot. They all flaunted the same sort of hairstyle—longish with a parting in the middle. A couple of them were carrying their shoes in their hands. Potu pointed to a bearded fellow. 'Must be the king, don't you think, Apuda?'

The very air, the sky, seemed to change colours at the arrival of the players. When Apu came back home that evening, bursting with excitement, he found his father sitting in the veranda busy writing something, and humming a line from a song. Apu thought his father was in such good spirits because he had come to know about the arrival of the jatra troupe. 'Five cart-loads of costumes and stuff, Baba! Oh!

There's never been anything like it! Such a troupe!' Apu informed his father with a flourish of his hands. Harihar looked up from his work: he had been writing verses of sacred text on special paper for amulets to be worn by his patron-clients. 'What costumes are you speaking of, my son?'

Apu was appalled! Was it possible that his father didn't know of the *most* momentous event in the village? He regarded his father with infinite pity.

The next morning Apu is obliged like every other day to sit down to his studies. After a bit he says tearfully, 'I want to go to Panchanan-tala . . . everybody's going, and am I to sit here all by myself and study? What if the jatra begins right away?'

'You must study now. You'll hear the drums when the jatra begins: you may go then,' says his father. Harihar has been away, working in distant places for the past few months. He is reluctant to part with his son when he is home for a few days between trips.

Apu sheds secret tears of rage and hurt as he begins once more to recite the mathematical formulae of Shubhankari in tearful drawling chants: 'If the monthly wages are such and such, daily wages would be how much?'

There is no performance in the morning. Word gets around that the jatra will begin later in the afternoon. Apu runs to his mother and describes to her in a weepy voice the tyrannical behaviour of his father. Sarbojoya goes to plead his case before her husband, 'Won't you let the boy go? It's the one day of the year. You're hardly home for nine months of the year anyway; is he going to turn into a Tarkalankar pandit in a single day?'

Apu is granted a holiday. He spends the entire afternoon at the community centre. Before the performance begins in the early evening he rushes off home for a quick meal. His father is still busy writing the amulets. On other days he is made to sit next to his father and read.

As he is about to set off Durga prods him, 'Apu, why don't you tell Ma that I'll be going to see the jatra too?'

So Apu asks his mother, 'Can't Didi come with me, Ma? They've marked off an enclosure for the girls with slatted matting and all—she can sit there.'

'Not now,' says his mother. 'I shall be going with the neighbours later and she can come with me.'

Just as he is on his way, Durga runs after him, 'Apu! Listen . . .' When he comes back to her she says smilingly, 'Put out your hand and shut your eyes.' When he does, she puts two paise on his palm and curls up his fingers over them. 'Buy yourself some candied rice, or if they sell litchis, treat yourself to some.'

Only a week ago Apu had secretly asked his sister, 'Didi, do you have any money in your doll's box? Will you give me a paisa?'

'What will you do with the money?' Durga wanted to know.

'I want to eat a litchi,' said Apu, glancing at his sister with his shy smile. He added by way of an explanation, 'They've put up a platform in Baishnab Garden and brought down a huge pile of litchis—two baskets full! They're selling them for six a paisa . . . such big ones too, flaming red! Satuda bought some and so did Sadhonda . . .' After a pause he asked her again, 'Do you have a paisa, Didi?'

But Durga's box was empty that day and she couldn't give him any money. She had felt very sad to see the little fellow turn away despondently. So the evening before she had wheedled some money from her father saying that she wanted some for Charak festivities. Her brother was precious as gold to her; she felt terribly sad when she wasn't able to satisfy his simplest wishes.

Apu skipped away. Their mother came back from the ghat and said, 'Dugga, will you do something for me . . . find me a couple of gandha bhedali leaves from Ranu's garden, will you? Apu hasn't been keeping too well: I'll make him a broth of the leaves.'

Durga promptly bounded off. She pushed her way through weeds and jungle as high as a man to look for the pungent leaves. She sang as she made her way, tossing her head in time to the rhythm. It was a verse she had heard her Pishima sing when she was still a child:

In forests gold and yellow,
Lost my nose-ring dear;
Lost my heart's desire . . .

18

Prince Ajay

The jatra began. Now there was no one in the world but Apu and the players of Neelmoni Hazra's troupe. No one else and nothing else. The various pieces followed each other in rapid succession. Such splendid costumes, such grand gestures!

Suddenly, a familiar voice behind him said, 'Khoka, can you see properly?' Apu did not know when his father had joined the spectators.

'Where's Didi?' he asked, turning around to talk to his father. 'Is she in the enclosure, Baba?'

But now as a result of the secret machinations of the minister, the king is exiled from his own kingdom. As he leaves for the forest with his wife and children the violin strikes up a dolorous note. In order to sustain the appropriate sentiment of pity and grief, the karuna rasa, for as long as possible, the king, holding the family members by their hands, pauses at every step. No real king on his way to a forest would have behaved in this fashion before a mass of assembled people were he not completely out of his mind. At the betrayal, the trusty Royal Commander-in-Chief is overtaken by a passion of rage exceeding any violent seizure.

Afraid to miss out on anything, Apu practically stops blinking. He is overwhelmed by all the goings on: he has never seen anything like it. For some time there was no trace of the king or the queen. In the deep dark forest there was only Prince Ajay and his sister, Princess Indulekha, and the wanderings of the pair. There is no one to look after them or show them the way. Indulekha goes off in search for fruits for her brother but she never comes back. Ajay keeps looking for his sister in the forest and suddenly, on the banks of a river, he stumbles upon Indulekha's body—driven by pangs of hunger she has died eating poisonous berries. Then follows a heart-rending song of Ajay's: 'Where have you gone my dearest companion, leaving me alone in the desolate forest?' Apu who has been watching with rapt attention cannot help but break into sobs at this point.

And then! A dazzling swordplay between Bichitraketu and the King of Kalinga—how awful and how fierce it was! Ohh! The gas lights will surely be smashed to smithereens or a helpless spectator blinded by the flashing blades! 'Watch out for the lights! The lights!' cry out members of the audience. But with amazing dexterity the warriors continue their duel and the lights are left unscathed. Whooh! Long live Bichitraketu!

In the course of the long passage where the chorus sings and the violinist shows off his virtuosity, Apu was gently nudged awake by his father. 'Do you want to go home, Khoka? Are you sleepy?'

Sleep? Never! He will never go home.

His father took him out of the seating enclosure and handed him two paise. 'Buy some food with this, Khoka. As for me, I'm heading home.' Apu had a strong impulse to buy one paisa worth of paan. There was quite a crowd near the paan stall and he pushed his way through to—an astonishing sight. The Commander-in-Chief Bichitraketu, his sword sheathed by his side, was puffing away at a cigarette. A massive crowd surged around him. And wonder upon wonders! Here was Prince Ajay himself, appeared out of nowhere it seems. He was tugging at Bichitraketu's elbow and saying, 'Kishorida, will you treat me to a paisa worth of paan?' There was no trace of any loyalty in the Commander-in-Chief's demeanour towards the prince as he shook him off unceremoniously. 'Get lost. Haven't got that kind of money. Didn't the two of you use up all my soap this morning, without as much as a by your leave too!'

Prince Ajay would not give up. 'Come on Kishorida, give us a treat. As though I've never treated you.' But Bichitraketu shook off his hand and walked away.

The prince was about the same age as Apu. He was a fair good-looking lad with a lovely singing voice. Apu looked at him admiringly, dying to make his acquaintance. Suddenly he found himself going up to him (something gave him courage) and saying shyly, 'Will you have a paan?'

'Will you treat me?' asked Ajay in surprise. 'Will you get me one, then?'

The two got talking and struck up a friendship. Well, not quite a friendship yet, for Apu was totally awestruck and dazed. *This* was the one he had been looking forward to for all these years—this Prince Ajay. All the hundreds of fairy tales that his mother had recounted, the thousand and one dream images of his childish imagination—in all of them he had longed for just such a being, with these very eyes, this face and such a voice. It was just as he had hoped and desired.

'Where do you live?' Ajay asked him. 'They've assigned me to a family for meals, but they eat very late. Which of us has been assigned to your family?'

Apu felt a delicious shiver of excitement. 'There is someone who comes to eat at our place. I saw him play the dholak today; but why don't you start coming instead from tomorrow . . . I shall come and bring you home. The dholak player can go to the house you were going to.'

After they had chatted and walked around for a bit, Ajay said, 'I must get back now. I've a song in the last scene, you know.'

Apu came back home in the last hours of the night after the jatra got over. On the way back, whatever he heard seemed to him a scene from the performance, an 'acto' from the jatra.

His sister shook him awake to ask him 'Apu! Apu, how was the jatra?' And Apu thought it was Princess Indulekha herself speaking from somewhere inside a deep dark forest, he was in such a dream world. He announced happily to his mother, 'You know, Ma, the one who was playing Prince Ajay—he's going to be coming for meals to our place from tomorrow.'

'Will there be two eating here then? How shall we manage two . . .'

'Well, can't we ask one to go away? Only Ajay need come here.'

'Apu, do tell me how it was . . .' asked Durga.

'Never seen anything like it. When the princess dies, such a song he sings!' Apu heard the wailing notes of the violin through the night as he lay half asleep on his bed. He woke up rather late, having gone to sleep late and then having barely slept. The sunlight pierced his eyes like needles. It hurt even when he splashed water on them. But he still heard the orchestra, the sound of the violin, the dholak and the cymbals, as though he was still seated in the jatra enclosure.

The neighbourhood girls were chattering on their way to the ghat—Apu believed that one was Dhirabati, another the Queen of Kalinga and the other Prince Ajay's mother, Basumati. As for his sister, every word she said, every gesture of hers . . . it was as if she were Princess Indulekha herself. The one who played Indulekha last night didn't do a bad job, but the image he had created of the princess was in the likeness of his sister. The same complexion, the same big eyes and lovely long hair like hers.

Apu brought Ajay home for the afternoon meal. His mother served the two boys and came to know something of Ajay's life. He was an orphan from a Brahmin family. He had been brought up by an aunt, but she was now dead. He had been working with the jatra troupe for a year now. Sarbojoya felt very drawn to the boy—she plied him with whatever food she had cooked. On his part, the boy ate the frugal meal with great contentment.

'Ma, why don't you ask him to sing that song ...' whispered Durga into her mother's ear. 'You know, the one which goes, "Where have you gone my dearest companion, leaving me alone in the desolate forest".'

Ajay gave a full-throated rendering of the song. Apu was spellbound and Sarbojoya's eyes filled with tears. Such a talented boy and motherless! He sang many more songs.

'I shall be roasting some rice later this afternoon,' she said to him, 'you must come and have some. Don't be shy; come whenever you feel like, it's your home—remember.'

Apu took his friend to the river. Once there, Ajay said, 'You have a very sweet voice. Why don't you sing me something?' Apu thought winning praise from such quarters would be quite special. He did wish to sing, but he was also afraid to sing before a singer from a jatra troupe. Finally, the two sat down under the big red silk-cotton tree in a secluded corner of the bamboo grove, a little distance away from the path along the river.

Apu had to struggle to overcome his shyness. He began with an old song from *Dashu Ray's Panchali* that he had heard his father sing: 'I rest at your feet my Lord, reveal yourself O Eternal One . . .' He had liked it enough to write down the words. 'What a lovely voice you have!' said Ajay in surprise when he was done. 'Why don't you have some singing lessons? Sing me another, will you?' Apu enthusiastically began a second song: 'Awaiting the crossing my heart dives into the day's end . . .' His sister had picked up the song from somewhere; Apu had learnt it from her in turn, attracted by the tune. When there was no one else at home brother and sister would sometimes sing it together. When he finished there was a burst of fresh praise from Ajay. 'I'm telling you, with a voice like that you can easily get fifteen rupees a month from any troupe . . . and if you were to train it a bit then—'

Apu had often asked Durga, when the two were by themselves at home, 'Didi, do you think I can sing? Am I musical?' His Didi had always encouraged him. But however encouraging she was, these words of praise from a professional and much awarded singer (Ajay had been gifted many medals by appreciative members of the audience) from a proper jatra company filled Apu with such bliss that he was quite speechless. 'Why don't you teach me your song?' he said after a while. Then they both sang it together.

Ajay, who had never before found such a companion, opened up his heart to Apu. He had saved up about forty rupees. Once he was a little older he would leave this company and join another troupe. The troupe leader here beat up people quite a bit. He would join Ashutosh Pal's company. Players had a good deal there he was told—they were even given hot luchis for dinner every night. And if you didn't wish to have meals with the company you got *three annas* to buy your own rations. Once he had left this troupe he would come back to Apu's home and spend a few days with the family.

It was still afternoon when Ajay said he had to leave. 'The show will begin early today,' said Ajay. 'If it's *Parashuram's Pride Vanquished* I shall be playing Niyati—there's a beautiful song that goes with the role . . .'

The jatra performed for another three days in the village. The villagers had nothing on their lips but talk of the jatra . . . the cowherd grazing his cows, the boatman on the river, and the people in the fields and along the paths . . . they all hummed tunes picked up from the troupe. The women began inviting the boy players home and had them sing their favourites; Apu too learnt several new songs. One day when he had gone to where the troupe was lodged, the players pressed him to sing something; he must 'oblige them' with a song, they said, as Ajay had just informed them that he was a good singer. After much pleading and cajoling Apu was at last persuaded to sing a song, to show his expertise. Then they took him to their employer, the Adhikari, and Apu had to sing another song for him. The Adhikari was a dark pot-bellied man who sang as part of the chorus during shows. When he had heard Apu, he said, 'Why don't you join the troupe, my boy?' Apu's heart swelled with pride and delight. The rest urged him to join as well. Apu wished he could sign up right away. It seemed absurd that until a few days ago he had not realized that the greatest good fortune for a human being was to work in a jatra company! He took aside Ajay and asked him, 'If I were to join the troupe now what parts would I be playing?'

'Well,' said his friend, 'to begin with you'd be playing a "lad" or a "girl" in the chorus and then after you've been trained up . . .'

Apu had no inclination to dress as a girl. All he wanted was to wear a golden crown on his head and have a sword by his side; like the Commander-in-Chief, he wanted to be part of a battle scene. Anyway, he would join up as soon as he was grown up for sure. This was the one and only aim in his life from now on.

After another five days, the contract with the village was over and the troupe was ready to leave. Ajay had become a familiar sight in their home. He dropped in whenever he could; he became like a brother to Apu. He was a boy, just like Sarbojoya's Apu, and had no one to call his own in the world. Sarbojoya had begun cherishing him the same way as she did her own son. Durga thought of him as another brother. She had learnt so many songs from him and heard stories and she in turn had told him stories about her aunt, her father's sister, whom she had loved dearly. The three children had drawn big squares in the courtyard to play hopscotch together. Whenever Ajay sat down to a meal, Durga had urged him to have some more. Until now, no one had cared if he had eaten or slept well—he had only been one of the many members of a professional touring company.

As he was about to leave Ajay suddenly opened his bundle and took out five rupees from his savings. He wanted to give it to Sarbojoya. 'To buy a nice sari for Didi when she gets married,' he explained awkwardly.

'No, my dear, that is not right. It is enough that you have expressed the desire . . . you will grow up, marry and have a family of your own . . . you will need the money,' said Sarbojoya. Ajay was unwilling to take it back but after much effort they persuaded him to put it back.

The family came up a little distance to see him off. 'You must send me a letter when Didi gets married,' Ajay said several times before leaving them.

His boyish figure disappeared behind the bushes of ghetu and sheora in the shadow of the big gaub tree and Sarbojoya was struck once more by how very young he was. 'Poor thing, he's had to take to the road for a living at such a tender age. If my Apu were to—God forbid!'

19

Ink shiny black

In the early years after Harihar had first returned from Kashi, everyone had predicted a radiant future for him. People spoke highly of his learning; it was said that no one in these parts was such a scholar and it was generally believed that he was 'bound to do something'. Sarbojoya too, believed that 'they' would invite her husband to take up a really worthy job. (Her notions as to *who* would invite him was as vague as the misty sea.) But all that was a long time ago. Months and years rolled by. The worm-eaten hinges and doors of their house fell into greater disrepair and the beams began to crack and hang perilously from the roof. Whatever little they possessed was falling apart. But Sarbojoya had not yet given up all hope. Every time Harihar came back from far-off places he would speak with such conviction of such promising situations, it seemed something splendid was imminent, and she would believe that they were on the brink of becoming well-off. But nothing ever happened.

This time it was over two months since Harihar had left. He had not sent any money home for a long time. Durga was constantly ill. She would be well for a few days and then suddenly the fever would come back again.

One day, during her wanderings, Durga found a small taro which she dug up carefully. She brought it to her mother and sat determinedly at the kitchen door with it, like someone fasting for a righteous cause—trying her best to persuade her mother to cook the taro.

'What is it with you, Dugga!' said her mother. 'Surely you don't expect to have any rice today—your fever came on even last evening.'

'But Ma, that wasn't really a fever—I was only feeling a little cold, that's all. Won't you cook me the taro with a little rice?'

'You've become quite greedy ever since you've been ill, always wanting to eat this and that. If you stay well today and all of tomorrow, I'll cook it for you the day after.'

Durga finally had to put away the taro when, despite all her pleas, she could not succeed in moving her mother. She sat quietly for a while. 'I'm doing quite well today,' she told herself, 'I'm not going to have any fever again. I'll have fried potatoes with roti in the evening . . .' Soon enough she began yawning. She knew by now that this was a prelude to the fever. But she comforted herself saying, 'The yawns don't mean a thing. People keep yawning anyway. I won't have any fever.' By and by she began shivering and wanted to sit in the sun. She stepped outdoors quietly, not wanting her mother to know. She felt hollow inside. 'Must be 'cause I've been worrying about the fever . . . I'm not really feverish,' she told herself. The bright sunshine fell on the mossy green wall of their house. Slowly, the shadows lengthened. If she tried thinking of other things, the fever would surely not come she believed. She called Apu, 'Come sit next to me, and we'll have a nice chat.' Before they were quite done with their chatting she was overtaken by a fit of fever; she went to bed, gathering her thin rag-quilt tightly around her.

Ever since their father has been away it's been hard getting hold of Apu. His books, writing materials, the low desk, now all but worm-eaten, are all gathering dust. He is off early in the morning with a pouch full of cowries and only comes back in the late afternoon in time for his meal.

'What's happening to the boy—he's left off studying altogether,' his mother grumbles and scolds. 'Just let him come home an' I shall tell him about what you've been up to!'

Frightened by the threat Apu sits down to study. He opens his books, scattering them all over the place. 'Ma, will you give me some catechu? I'll put some in the inkpot.' He writes up pages of handwriting and puts them out in the sun. When they dry, the catechu-ink begins to shine. Apu regards the gleaming letters with delight and thinks, 'I'll put a little more of the catechu tomorrow . . . ooh! its shining like anything.' The next time he picks up a huge lump of catechu from his mother's paan box without telling her and puts it into the inkpot. Then, after he has done his writing, he gazes avidly at the letters to see how much more they are gleaming today. He wonders, 'What if I were to put in some more today . . .'

He was finally caught by his mother one day. 'He's left off studying,' she said, 'but look at the boy—wasting huge lumps of catechu every day! Put it all back!'

'How *can* one have good ink without catechu?' said Apu, embarrassed at being caught, but standing his ground. 'Can I just make ink—?'

'Indeed! How can one make ink without any catechu—all the other boys everywhere, as though they never do any studying! You'd think they have tons of catechu waiting for them in the shops!'

Apu was writing a play. He had almost filled up his notebook with his writing: The minister's treachery has forced the king into exile in the forest. Prince Neelambar and Princess Amba are captured by robbers. A fierce battle follows and the princess is discovered by the bank of a river, dead. A complex character called Satu also makes an appearance in the play and is sentenced to death despite the absence of any specific villainy on his part. At the end of the play the Princess Amba is restored to life by the grace of the sage Narada, and is married off to the trusty minister Jibanketu . . . and such like details follow.

There was a certain book that they had called *Charitmala*, about the lives of famous people. It was written by Ishwarchandra Vidyasagar. It was an old book, one of the many that his father may have brought home from some strange place. Harihar collected books for his son in the course of his travels. Apu liked leafing through the book and reading over and over again the parts he fancied . . . Whenever Roscoe, the farmer's son, was sent to the market to sell potatoes he would stop by a fence and do algebra. Lacking paper, he would work out sums on pieces of leather, using a blunt awl to inscribe the figures . . . And Duval the cowherd would let the cattle graze wherever they pleased while he sat absorbed in texts of maps. Apu wanted to be like the boys in the book. But what was 'algebra'? He wanted to study 'algebra' as Roscoe did. He didn't care for the kind of handwriting he had to practise or the sort of mathematical systems like the Shubhankari that he was expected to learn. He would rather sit down in the quiet shady woods, under a tree or by a fence and read books on 'maps' (what was *that*?) and all sorts of heavy books and become a learned scholar. But where would he get hold of these things? These books on cartography, algebra or Latin grammar? His mother might scold him, but he didn't have here what he really wished to study.

20

Fishes in the bamboo grove

The rain kept falling. It stopped for a bit and then started again with such force that the spray created a misty world. Harihar had sent only five rupees home, and that was quite some time ago. There had been no money or a letter since. Sarbojoya awoke every morning hoping that surely today the household expenses would come to her. 'You are always playing, Apu,' she rebuked her son one day, 'so you miss him. You must sit beside the letterbox. You must catch the peon as soon as he comes and ask him if there's a letter.'

'But I *do* sit right there,' protested Apu. 'Putu's family got a letter yesterday; ask him if you don't believe me. How can you say I'm never there?'

The rains had now begun in earnest. Apu sat waiting near the Rays' family temple watching out for the peon. He was afraid of the thunder that rolled in the sky. When the lightning flashed he felt the gods must be in a rage. Oh! It's going to come crashing any moment now! He shut his eyes tightly and stopped his ears with his fingers. When he came back home he found that his mother and his sister had been out all afternoon in the rain; both were wet to the skin. They had come back with armloads of kochu greens which were now lying in a heap near the kitchen.

'Where did you bring them from, Ma? What an awful lot you've brought!' said Apu.

'A lot!' said Durga with a laugh. 'Huh! It's great fun for you to be sitting around and doing nothing, isn't it? There, by the jamun tree, that big body of water . . . this much water—right up to the knees we waded! Want to try?'

The next morning, on the way to the ghat, Sarbojoya met the barber's wife. She took out a bell-metal plate from the folds of her sari and said, "See, here it is . . . solid stuff . . . nothing cheap about it—full bell-metal. You'd said you would . . . I thought let me talk to her, it's not just any old thing you know—it came with me from my parents as part of my dowry. You won't get this sort any more . . .'

After much bargaining the barber's wife put away the plate in the folds of her sari and gave Sarbojoya half a rupee for it. Sarbojoya begged her several times to keep the sale a secret.

For the next couple of days it rained in torrents. The east wind blew in fierce gusts and the hollows and ditches in the village were soon overflowing. People had to wade through knee-deep water to get anywhere. Day and night the storm whistled through the bamboo grove and the bamboos swayed and keeled over, almost touching the ground. For five days it went on in the same way. All one could hear was the sound of the storm and the unceasing rain.

Then one day, Apu ran up the steps to their raised veranda and hurriedly wiping his head dry, called out to his sister, 'Didi, do come and see—the water's come right up to our bamboo grove!'

Durga, who was lying bundled up in her rag-quilt, didn't get up; she merely asked, 'How far has the water come up, Apu?'

'You must go out and see for yourself tomorrow, once your fever comes down. It's almost up to the knees by the tamarind tree. Where's Ma?' he wanted to know.

There was not a grain of cereal at home, only a handful of roasted rice gone stale. Apu had a fit of weeping, 'No, I shan't eat that—don't you think I'm hungry—I want some rice, aaanh . . .'

'My precious, my sweet,' his mother soothed him, 'you mustn't cry, I'll give you lots of roasted rice. Don't you see I can't cook—all the water's got into the stove.' She carefully took out something from her sari. It was a fish. 'Look at what I have—a koi . . . I found it walking on its gills by the bamboo grove,' she said with a smile. 'With all the rain and the flooding, they're floating up from the canal. The river and the Borajpota Lake have become one, you see . . . so the fish are just flowing along.'

Now Durga pushed aside her rag-quilt. 'Ma, let me have a look at the fish! Ma, do koi really walk around on their gills? Are there any more of 'em?'

Apu was about to dart off in the pouring rain to look for more; his mother persuaded him with great difficulty to wait till the rain stopped.

'When I'm a little better, let's go Apu, and we'll bring back fish from the bamboo grove first thing in the morning,' said Durga. She wondered at this magical event—fishes in the bamboo grove! How did they ever get there? What fun! But did Ma look hard enough? She would've found more had she searched well . . . couldn't get to see how they walk on their gills . . . must go tomorrow . . . my fever will be gone tomorrow . . . I'll be fine . . .

Evening fell around them darkening the surrounding jungle. The darkness was everywhere, with the overcast evening sky and a thirteen-day-old moon.

Apu and his mother are sitting on a corner of the bed that Durga is lying on. Brother and sister get into a fierce argument. Apu moves over to his mother and nestles up to her: 'It gets so shivery when the cold wind blows.' Then he laughs as he asks his mother, 'How does that rhyme go, Ma? The one about "Dark chilli grinding spices, hair strewn on the floor"?'

'In the meantime Ma's left the land ever more,' chips in Durga.

'Huh! Is that so? Is it really "In the meantime Ma's left

the land ever more"?' Apu asks his mother, laughing at his sister's ignorance.

Sarbojoya finds his innocent laughter painful—it bites into her like a wound. 'I have only this one son, not seven, not five. Such misfortune have I brought into the world with his birth that I can't fulfil his least desire! It's not ghee or luchi or sandesh he wants—all he wants is a handful of rice.' And she dreams, 'this broken-down house and a household where there's never enough . . . once my Apu becomes a man, all my sorrows will be over. May God make a man of him!'

Late that night Sarbojoya was awakened by cries from Apu. 'Ma, get up, won't you get up, Ma? I'm getting wet.'

Sarbojoya got up and lit the lamp. She heard the rain outside, loud and heavy. The roof was leaking . . . there was water dripping everywhere. She moved the bedding and spread it on a dry patch in the room. Durga was asleep, in the grip of a high fever. Her mother put out her hand to find that her rag-quilt was sopping wet. 'Dugga, O Dugga,' she called her gently, 'wake up for a bit, dear, I'll move the bedding. Dugga, quick—everything is drenched.'

Even after the children had fallen asleep Sarbojoya could not go to sleep. The night was dark and the rain poured without a pause. She had a premonition . . . she was afraid something was about to happen. She was trembling. 'And what could've happened to him . . .' she brooded. 'Forget the money, but not even a letter? It has never happened like this before . . . is he well?' Right away she made a vow to Goddess

Siddheswari, 'Ma, I shall make you an offering of food worth five annas and a paisa, bring me some good news, O Mother.'

The rain let up for a bit the next morning. When Sarbojoya came out of their home she found the little hollow in the bamboo grove brimming with water. On the path to the ghat she came upon Nibaron's mother hurrying off somewhere in wet clothes. 'Nibaron's Ma,' she called out, 'I'd like a word with you. You had told me once . . .' she began in embarrassment, '. . . you wanted a shawl for your son—the kind you get in Vrindavan—would you like it now?'

'D'ye have one?' asked Nibaron's Ma. 'Let it clear a bit an' I'll bring my son 'long. Is it new, Mother, or is it an old 'un you're talking of?'

'You'll see for yourself as soon as you come. It is a bit old, but no one's ever used it; it was washed and kept away.' After a pause she added, 'Do you thresh any paddy these days?'

'D'you think paddy will dry in such wet weather? I've just set aside a bit o' rice for my own use.'

'Why don't you bring me . . . a few measures of the rice anyway?' Sarbojoya's voice became low and pleading. 'You see, I simply can't get anyone to buy me some rice from the market. I've been going around with the money but there's not a body willing to fetch it for me. I'm in such trouble, my dear.'

Nibaron's mother agreed to get the rice. 'Be coming along with it soon,' she promised. 'But the paddy is the coarse kind—would the likes of you be able to digest it, Mother?'

Durga was unable to swallow any more of the bitter concoction of neem bark. The fever remained much the same. There was no medicine, no nourishing food, no doctor for her. She asked her mother, 'Will you have a paisa worth of biscuits fetched for me . . . something salty? They taste really nice.'

It was not even possible to give her barley . . . and biscuits!

The rain started again later in the afternoon and with it came the storm. It was as though a fierce storm would always rage whenever it rained. The rain fell with a thunderous rhythm of its own and the east wind hissed and screamed. The water rose and flowed over and into everything. Lowering rain clouds sped across the sky blotting out the light of the September evening. You couldn't hear a thing excepting for the massive drumming of the rain. The creaky windows and doors falling on their hinges let in sharp sprays with gusts of the cold wind. How could mere bits of sacking and rags stuffed into the holes and gaping spaces of the broken-down house withstand such demonic force!

After midnight when both the children had fallen asleep, the rain came down even harder. Sarbojoya could not sleep; she sat up. She was weak from worry and hunger and her head was spinning. The room was awash in sheets of rain. She put out her hand to touch Apu and found he was soaking wet. What was she to do? How much of the night remained? She lit the little kerosene lamp, fumbling for the matches among the bedclothes. 'Apu, O Apu,' she called, 'get up, won't you!' To Durga she said, 'Dugga, move over, turn the other side . . . it's too wet here.'

Apu got up and looked around bleary eyed, then fell asleep again. There was a deafening crash outdoors. Sarbojoya ran to the door to peer outside. It looked strangely empty in the direction of the bamboo grove. The kitchen wall had collapsed. She could see straight through where it once stood. She shuddered. What if the old house were to . . .? Who would she call? Who would answer her call? She prayed frantically, 'Dear Lord, let this night pass safely, Lord, be merciful to the little ones . . .'

It had not yet dawned. The storm had calmed down but it was still drizzling. Neelmoni Mukherjee's wife was heading outdoors to check on the condition of the cowsheds when she heard a sharp and insistent knocking on the backdoor. 'Is that you daughter-in-law, at this time?' she said in astonishment as she opened the backdoor.

'Didi, will you call Foni's father? Will you ask him to come over to our place right away? Dugga is behaving strangely,' said Sarbojoya.

'Dugga! Why, what's happened to Dugga?' asked Neelmoni Mukherjee's wife.

'She's been down with fever for some time now, it's been comin' and goin'—malaria. The fever has shot up since last evening and you know there never was a night like last night. Hurry, please ask him . . .'

There was such a helpless and vulnerable look in Sarbojoya's eyes that Neelmoni Mukherjee's wife tried her best to reassure her. 'Don't you worry. You just stand here and wait a bit, I'll go and fetch him right away. I'll come along as well. The roof of the cowshed collapsed last night . . . such a terrible night it was, never seen anything like it . . . He went to sleep quite late—he'd got up before dawn to move the cows to safety. I'll call him now.'

A little later, Neelmoni Mukherjee, his wife and his elder son, Foni, and his two daughters all went over to Apu's.

Apu was seated next to Durga. 'What is it, my lad?' asked Neelmoni Mukherjee of Apu whose face showed signs of great distress.

'Didi's been babbling away,' the boy replied.

'Let's take a look at the pulse,' said Neelmoni Mukherjee, sitting down next to Durga. 'Hmm, the fever's still very high. Don't worry. Foni, run over to Nawabganj, go directly to Sharad Doctor and bring him back with you . . . Durga, O Durga . . .' he called out several times, but there was no response—she lay in a stupor.

Later that day, Sharad Doctor examined the patient and prescribed medicines. Her condition wasn't very critical, he said. 'It's the fever that has gone up.' He recommended that wet bandages be applied to her forehead to bring down the temperature. No one knew where Harihar was at present but a letter was posted to his old address.

The following day the storm blew over and the rain stopped. Slowly, the sky began to clear. Neelmoni Mukherjee came over twice a day to supervise the treatment. But the very next day, Durga's fever shot up once again. Sharad Doctor felt uneasy and thought it was a bad case. Another letter was sent off to Harihar.

Apu sat beside his sister, changing the wet strips of cloth on her forehead. 'Didi, Didi,' he called her a couple of times, 'do listen, Didi! Say something . . .'

Durga was in the same sort of daze as before. Her lips moved, she seemed to be saying something to herself soundlessly. Apu tried putting his ears to her lips every now and then, but he wasn't able to make out the words.

The fever left her late that afternoon. After a long time, Durga was able to open her eyes and she tried to look around her. She had become very weak and spoke in a thin quavering voice; you had to strain to hear her.

Apu kept sitting by his sister's side, even after their mother had left to attend to her housework. Durga turned her gaze on Apu, 'What time of the day is it, Apu?'

'It's not too late in the day,' he said. 'Do you see Didi, how nicely the sun's come out today! There's sunlight still on the top of our coconut tree.'

The two were silent for a while. Apu was thrilled at the sun which had come out after so many days of rain and wind. He kept gazing at the rosy tips of the tree, still lit up by the sun.

'Listen, Apu,' said Durga, after some time. 'There's something . . .'

'What is it, Didi?' He brought his face even closer to his sister's face.

'When I'm better, Apu, will you show me a train?'

'Sure, I will—once you get better. I'll ask Baba to take all of us by train and we'll go bathe in the Ganga.'

Another day and another night passed. It seemed as though there had never been a storm or any rain ever. The dazzling autumn sunshine filled the air.

It was about ten in the morning. Neelmoni Mukherjee, who had not been able to go bathe in the river because of the stormy weather, had just sat down for an oil massage, when he heard his wife call him in urgent tones, 'Will you come this way, quick? I seem to hear sounds of wailing from Apu's . . .'

They all ran to find out what had happened.

Sarbojoya was bent over her daughter crying out pitifully, 'Dugga, darling, look up, do look up once, O Dugga, call out to your mother . . . just once.'

'Let me see,' said Neelmoni Mukherjee entering the room. 'Move away. Move away please . . . why do you crowd around her, blocking off the fresh air!'

Sarbojoya forgot the propriety due to her neighbour who was to be honoured as an elder brother-in-law. 'What has befallen me!' she cried out. 'She doesn't speak. Why does she not look at me?'

Durga did not open her eyes any more to the light on earth.

Sharad Doctor was summoned again. He looked at the patient and said, 'There was a remission of the fever after the high temperature—her heart failed. Just the other day at the Mukherjees in Dasghara village, we had exactly the same case . . .'

Within half an hour the courtyard was a sea of people.

21

Welcoming the Goddess Durga

Harihar had not received the letters from home.
This time after he had left home, Harihar Ray had first gone to Gowari Krishnanagar. He did not know anyone there, but he had been enticed by the thought that it was a town with a big bazaar; something or the other was bound to turn up. He was then told that the town lawyers and the local landlords often hired Brahmin priests on a daily or monthly contract to recite verses to Goddess Chandi. Clutching on to this hope, he eked out for a fortnight on the meagre rations he had brought with him; but nothing turned up.

He was in deep trouble. He was a stranger to the place: there was no one he could look to for a paisa worth of help. When his money ran out he had to move out of the room he had rented at the bazaar. Someone told him of the local

Harisabha which gave shelter and food to the needy Brahmin traveller, but he found it to be a difficult place. He was given a place to sleep in, but a group of idle addicts had made it their haunt and they passed the entire night in great revelry, smoking weed and conversing loudly. Harihar endured it all in order to make the rounds of the wealthy lawyers and other potential patrons during the day. Coming back late, he would find on many a night that someone had dragged away his bedding and was happily snoring away on it. Harihar spent many of these nights sleeping outside on the veranda. When this became a regular occurrence, he had a somewhat sharp exchange of words with some of the addicts. They must have gone and said things about him to the secretary of the organization the very next morning. He was summoned by the latter and informed that they had a rule that no one could enjoy the hospitality of their Harisabha for more than three days, so he had better look out for another place. By evening Harihar was obliged to put together his belongings and leave the premises.

When he came to a quiet spot by the Khorey River he put down his bundle and sat down to refresh himself with splashes of water. He had not eaten the whole day. Sometime during the day he earned a rupee from a timber merchant: he had sat down next to a warehouse and sung a song to Shyama the dark goddess. At the end of the song the owner had given him a rupee as a token of respect. Harihar now changed the rupee to buy a few paise worth of puffed rice and curd from the bazaar, but it was hard getting the food down his throat. He had left home with money enough for the family to buy ten days of rations. It was now over two months—he hadn't been able to send them a single paisa. How were they managing? Apu had repeatedly told him that he should get him a copy of the *Padma Purana*. The boy loved reading. Harihar knew quite well that the boy often opened up his desk and leafed through his pile of books. Some time ago, Harihar had borrowed a copy of the *Padma Purana* in popular verse from a cheap bookstall in the neighbourhood. Apu wouldn't let go of the copy. He read it every day; he especially liked the bit about how Shiva had gone fishing. 'You must give me back the book, son,' Harihar would tell him from time to time, 'the owners want it back.' Only after he had made his father promise that he would buy him a new copy of the *Padma Purana*, did Apu agree to give up the book. A dozen or more times he had reminded Harihar: 'Baba, you *must* buy the book for me this time, absolutely, ab-so-lute-ly.' Durga had not set her sights too high—she had asked for a thin green sari and some nice red lac dye for ornamenting her feet. But these were elusive objects at the moment; his only thought was, how was his family managing their daily life?

When evening fell Harihar went back to the familiar woodpile for shelter. He did not sleep well that night. He tossed and turned wondering how he could send something home. Next morning he began wandering aimlessly once more. But perhaps his luck was about to turn at last for it was here, in Rakshit moshai's warehouse, that he came to know about a possible job. A wealthy moneylender in a village near Krishnanagar was looking for a priest who would undertake the duties of daily worship on a permanent basis. Rakshit moshai made the necessary contacts and the prospective employer also took a fancy to him. Harihar was given a nice room to live in and was looked after very well.

He had hardly worked for a few days when it was Durga Puja. His new employer gave Harihar ten rupees as a gift due to a Brahmin as well as travel expenses to visit home. When he stopped on his way at Rakshit moshai's in Gowari, the latter also gave him five rupees. Harihar bought clothes for his wife and children at the Ranaghat bazaar. Durga liked wearing red-bordered saris; he spent a lot of time choosing a nice one for her as well as several packets of red lac for her feet. Despite his best efforts, he was unable to get Apu his *Padma Purana*; instead, he bought him an illustrated copy of *The Greatness of Chandi or The Story of Kalketu* at a price of six annas. Sarbojoya had asked him to get some household items including a wooden rolling pin and so on—he got her all of those.

It was late afternoon by the time he had walked his way to the village from the nearest railway station. He hardly met anyone on the way. Besides, he was practically racing homewards without taking any real notice of the passers-by.

'Look at that!' he muttered as he came to the door. 'The

bamboos have completely keeled over the wall. And Uncle Bhubon never wanting to get them cut . . . what a mess!' Then, entering the inner courtyard, he cried out eagerly as he always did, 'My Dugga, my Apu . . . where are you?'

Sarbojoya came out of the house at the sound of his voice. 'All well at home?' Harihar asked her with a gentle smile. 'Where are they? Not at home?'

'Come in,' said Sarbojoya in a calm voice, moving forward to take the heavy bundle off her husband's hands. Although Harihar was struck by her unnatural calmness, he was not unduly disturbed. His imagination was in full flow thinking how the two would come rushing in any moment now: Dugga would ask with her smile, 'What have you brought for me, Baba?' And he would immediately open up the bundle and give her the sari and the packets of red lac, then take out the illustrated copy of *The Greatness of Chandi or The Story of Kalketu* and the tin train he had bought for Apu: they would both be thrilled. 'I've got you a nice wooden set of rolling pin and plate,' he said, as he entered the room. Then after he had looked around eagerly, he said in a slightly disheartened tone, 'Apu and Dugga— have they gone outdoors then?'

Sarbojoya could not control herself any more. She broke down in loud sobs, 'Is Dugga with us any more? She's cheated us and left us forever. Where have you been all this time?'

The Durga Puja at the Gangulys' was an old tradition.

This time too, Dinu the shehnai player from Ashmali

village came to play, just as he did on other years. The early morning air resounded joyously with the notes of the shehnai playing the welcoming agomoni—sounding the prelude to the arrival of Goddess Durga.

Harihar set off on an invitation to the Gangulys with his boy who was dressed in his new clothes. On the way he became absent minded. 'Come, my boy,' he told Apu. 'It is getting late.'

22

Nishchindipur

Actually, Apu hadn't really fallen asleep, he was awake. He heard every word of the conversation that his father and mother had that night while he lay there with his eyes shut. They were to leave this land of theirs and go to Kashi. His father was telling her of the many wonderful things that were there in Kashi, much better than anything here. He had lived there when he was young, knew all the people there, had many friends. People knew him and respected him in that ancient city. Besides, it was cheaper. His mother was also enthusiastic about going away—yes, those were lands of gold . . . no one ever knew what want was like, whereas here, it was only grief and sorrow all twelve months of the year. You only had to pluck up enough courage and get there, and your sorrows would be over. If his mother could, she would have left that very day; she did not wish to stay on for a single extra day. Finally, it was decided that they would leave in May.

In early May Harihar began making preparations to uproot themselves from their native village. Most of their possessions they wouldn't be able to take along with them, so these he sold to pay off all kinds of petty debts. A huge bed, an almirah and many low stools made of the solid wood of the jackfruit tree—they had many of these in their home. People came from all over to buy off the furniture at very cheap rates.

The village elders paid a visit to Harihar trying to dissuade him. They spoke eloquently on the plentifulness of fish and milk in Nishchindipur and the little money that one needed to run a household. They even improvised a comparative inventory of expenses on the spot to prove how much cheaper it was to live in Nishchindipur. Rajkrishna moshai was the only one from the village who had a different perspective. When he came to invite the family to his wife's Savitri-vrata, he discussed the move at some length before he said, 'Well, I don't see that there's anything to keep you here. Besides, if you stick to one place, stagnating in the mud, you become narrow minded, you shut yourself from the wide world. As for me, I've been thinking of a trip to Chandranath . . . God willing!'

Ranu came to their place when she heard the news. 'Is it true, Apu, that you will really leave the village and go elsewhere?

'It's true,' said Apu. 'Ask Ma.'

Ranu was still not convinced. After it was confirmed by Sarbojoya she was taken aback. She called Apu out to the courtyard and asked him, 'When will you be leaving?'

'Wednesday after next.'

'And will you never come back?'

Ranu had tears in her eyes. 'But don't you always say that there's never another village like Nishchindipur? No river, no fields like these . . . How will you be able to leave all this and go away?'

'What can I do, Ranudi?' said Apu. 'It wasn't I who spoke of leaving! It's Baba who wishes to settle in Benares; we can hardly get by here, you know.'

At the bathing ghat, Apu met Potu and they had a long talk. Potu did not know anything about their leaving Nishchindipur; he looked downcast at the news. 'You know how I went into the water just for you and worked so hard to clear all the weeds and cut a pit for you and all . . . and won't you be trappin' fish in it even once?'

This time around, Ramnavami, Dole, Charak and Goshtobehar—all the festival days came in a row. It was the time of the year which usually had Apu bursting with happiness. His sister and he practically abandoned everything else to enjoy each of the festivals to their heart's content.

On the day of Charak Puja Old Aturi died. Her double-thatched hut stood on the edge of the field to which the Charak fair had lately been shifted. Drawn by the crowd that had already gathered around the hut, Apu too went to have a look. Once, when he was little, he remembered he had been so terrified of her that he had run wildly, breaking through bamboo thickets and thorny scrub. It was funny to think that he had once been so scared of her. Now he felt that Old Aturi was neither a witch nor a demoness. She had simply lived all by herself in the outskirts of the village—an ugly old woman, helpless and alone—she had no son or daughter or anyone to take care of her. Had she any kith or kin would she have been lying dead in her house for a whole day, with no one to take her body to the pyre? Panchu fisherman's son brought out a clay pot he had found inside her hut and upturned it—a heap of dried mango powder fell out. The old woman used to pick up the fallen mangoes and make sun-dried mango strips and spicy mango powder which she would then sell at various weekly markets. That was how she survived. Apu had seen her selling her wares at the last big fair that was held at the time of the Chariot festival.

The Charak festival rang strangely hollow this time. Last year at the Charak fair Didi had been so happy buying a new painted pata. He remembered they had had a fight that morning. In the evening she had said to him, 'Apu, I'll give you some money, will you get me a pata with a painting of the "Abduction of Sita" from the fair?'

'A lot of mealy-mouthed stuff you want to buy!' he had

said, to take revenge. 'I can't get it for you. Why can't you buy one showing Rama and Ravana at war?'

'All you care for is war,' his sister had said. 'Just like a boy! Why, what's so bad about pata pictures of gods and goddesses?' Apu had never much respect for his sister's aesthetic sense.

Now he remembered her face when the fencing around their house blossomed with red rangchita and when the birds sang; the swaying of the fresh buds of the or-kalmi made him long for his sister. He could run up to her and say whatever he pleased and she would be delighted by him . . . where had she gone to . . . so far away? Would she never ever come back to play with the world that she had left behind?

There were brightly dressed peasant children from neighbouring villages, a young wife wearing a stiff new sari, a whole lot of folk, lines of them—all coming back from the Charak fair. Young boys were playing on their flute as they walked home. People had come from afar to the Goshtobehari fair, even as far as ten miles away. Each one was carrying back something or the other—a bird made of the white pith of shola, a wooden doll, a brightly coloured paper fan, a painted pot—all the things they had bought in the fair. Chinibash Baishnab had set up a stall for fritters at the fair: Apu had bought two paise worth of fries from his shop and was walking back home. He was wondering if they had a fair like this one at the place they were moving to.

Perhaps there would never be another Charak fair he could go to. He thought, if they don't have a fair at Charak I shall tell my father, 'Baba, I want to go to the fair, let me go to Nishchindipur; I could stay for a couple of days at Auntie's, couldn't I?'

The day after Charak, they started putting together all their belongings. Tomorrow, after their mid-day meal, they would be on their way.

In the evening his mother was making him hot parathas, as he sat in the veranda in front of the kitchen. The fronds of the coconut palm in their Uncle Neelmoni's garden glistened in the moonlight. Apu was filled with melancholy and a sense of loss as he looked that way. The closer it got to the day of departure, the enthusiasm he had had so far about going to a new place ebbed away. Instead, the imminent separation gave birth to a deep pain inside him; it played like a note of sorrow in his mind.

This house of theirs, the bamboo thicket there, the mango orchard at Shaltey-khagi, the riverbank and that spot where he and his sister had the cookout—how deeply he loved them all. Would there be such a coconut tree where they were going? From the earliest moments of his conscious life he could remember the coconut tree standing right there. How beautiful the fronds looked in the moonlight. How often he had played cards with his Didi late into the night, right here on the veranda, watching the moonlight fall like a shower from the swaying palm fronds. How often he had felt that this Nishchindipur of theirs was the most beautiful place . . . Would there be a tree on the fringes of the jungle like that next to the kitchen veranda in their new home? Would he be able to fish, pick up mangoes, row a boat and play at trains? Would the new place have a ghat like the one at Kadam-tala? And a Ranudi? And a field like Sonadanga? Were they not happy here—why leave it all for nothing?

23

I remember

Something happened that afternoon. His mother was away attending the Savitri-vrata ritual at their neighbour's and his father was sleeping after the midday meal. Apu was going through the odds and ends stored on the shelf along the crossbeam of the room, figuring out what he would take with him and what had to stay. His rummaging overturned a small earthen pitcher; a little object rolled out of it and fell on the floor. Apu picked it up and looked at it with shocked surprise. It was covered with cobwebs and had gone mouldy, but it was easy enough to make out what it was—that little golden casket which was stolen last year from Shejo bou's house.

For a long time Apu stood absentmindedly with the little casket in his palm. In the silence and loneliness of the scorching May afternoon, the whistling and moaning of the bamboos came to his ears like a distant call. 'Poor Didi must have stolen the casket and hidden it inside the pitcher,' he said to himself.

He thought for a bit and slowly walked towards the backdoor. The bamboo thickets were drowsing in the midday heat for as far as he could see. The shrill long-drawn-out cries of the familiar kite perched on a tree top came to his ears. It was the very afternoon of ancient times—of the unfortunate defeated princes of the Mahabharata, fugitives now at the Dwaipayan Lake. Apu stood there for some moments and in one quick movement flung the golden casket into the dense thicket of bamboos. 'It will lie there . . . no one will ever know of anything,' he thought. 'Who will ever go that way!'

Apu did not speak of the golden casket to anyone, not even to his mother.

Later that afternoon Hiru driver and his bullock cart trundled off with the family.

There had been some clouds visible in the morning sky but they had vanished long before ten o'clock and now the fierce May sun seemed to be raining fire on the trees and on the fields and on the path. Potu walked along with their cart for as long as he could. 'You know, Apuda,' he said, 'a really good jatra troupe has been contracted this time . . . you'll be missing the plays!'

'Will you take an extra leaflet for me about the plays they will put on—send it to me, will you?' said Apu.

Once more the road wound its way past the big field where the Charak fair was held every year. Empty halves of green coconut shells were strewn across the field. Some people had made a fire for cooking; all that remained now was a heap of scorched mud and a blackened pot.

Harihar sat in silence. He was filled with disquiet: were they doing the right thing by leaving? Their home had been settled by his ancestors ages ago, the house next to theirs had long crumbled in ruins, but even the little earthen lamp that was lit every evening in their home was to be forever extinguished from this evening. How would his father, the late Pandit Ramchand Tarkalankar, be looking upon this act of his son?

For as long as he could, Apu stared unblinkingly at the last house on the fringe of the village—Old Aturi's double-thatched hut. The cart went past a big garden of date-palms before it turned and climbed up to the main road that led to Ashadu.

As they reached the end of the village, Sarbojoya thought, 'We're leaving behind us all the shame and humiliation, the poverty and the want—whatever has dogged us all these years. Ahead of us lies a new life, new prosperity and hope . . .'

The cart reached the station around ten at night. Apu, who had long been awaiting this moment, jumped off the cart as soon as it came to a halt and bounded up to the railway platform. The eight-thirty train had passed long ago. He had found out from his father that there would be no more trains coming in that night. All because of those two ancient bullocks of Hiru driver's! He would surely have seen at least one train otherwise.

A huge bale of tobacco lay trussed up on the platform. Two men from the railways were pressing the tobacco bundles in a machine that looked like an iron box with extraordinarily long handles. The metal rails glistened in the moonlight. On one side of the tracks stood a long pole with two red lights and on this side too, were two red lights on another pole. Inside the station room a four-legged oil lantern was alight; a pile of bound books and papers sat next to it. Apu ventured to the door and peeped in. He watched the station babu go tap-tapping on something that looked like a small knob.

Istishun . . . istishun . . . soon, very soon, tomorrow morning, he would not only see a train but he would actually get inside one!

He didn't feel like budging from the platform. But his father came to call him. The thing that seemed made of little knobs was called a telegraph machine, his father explained. Apu turned back to the platform and found that preparations were on for cooking the evening meal by the pond next to the station. Another cart had been standing there before theirs had come. Amongst the travellers were a nineteen-year-old married woman and a young man. Apu heard that the woman was of the Biswas family in Habibpur; her brother was escorting her on a visit to the parental home. His mother and the young wife were already chatting away like old acquaintances. Sarbojoya was washing the rice and dal for the khichdi while the younger woman was peeling the potatoes—the meal was to be cooked together.

Their train arrived at seven-thirty the next morning. Apu had been standing on the edge of the platform staring ahead, waiting with bated breath for the train. 'Don't lean forward like that, son,' cautioned Harihar, 'come away to this side.' A porter was busy shouting at people to move away from the platform edge.

Goodness! What a long thing it was! And what a frightful racket it was making! Was that what they called an 'injin'—that huge black car right in front belching smoke and fire? Oh! What a tremendous sight!

The young woman from Habibpur drew aside the sari covering her head to stare at the incoming train. With a great deal of shouting and jostling all their possessions were loaded on the train. Inside, he saw wooden benches facing each other. The floor looked like it was made of cement. Exactly like a room it was, with windows and doors and everything.

Apu could not believe that this monstrous thing which had stopped at the platform would once again move. Who knows, perhaps it would not be able to move, perhaps they might announce just now, 'Listen all, get off the train please, our train will not run today.'

A man with a bundle of thatch-grass on his head stood on the other side of the wire fencing waiting for the train to go. Apu looked upon him with compassion—to think that the poor fellow was not getting on to the train, what a waste of one's life!

Hiru driver stood on the other side of the gate gaping at the train.

The train moved. What a strange and marvellous shaking and swaying! In a flash, Majherpara station, the people and the tobacco bales on the platform, Hiru driver staring open-mouthed at them, everyone and everything, had been left behind and the train was now rushing past the Ulukhar Field. The trees and bushes simply shot past the windows on either side—what speed! This is what they called a train. Ohh! It seemed as if the world was whirling around them. Trees, bushes, the small huts of peasants, thatched lean-tos all blurred in his gaze. Beneath them there was a monotonous sound of heavy grinding metal and what an infernal noise the engine in front was making!

That day when he and his Didi had set out to look for the missing calf and had run breathlessly across fields and ditches to glimpse the railroad . . . That day and today . . .?

There, beneath the sky where stood the file of trees along the brick road to Ashadu-Durgapur, beyond that, in that direction, where their village path took a bend and climbed up to Sonadanga Field, there, right there by the old jamun tree at the end of the village stood his sister looking wistfully at their train. No one had brought her along, she had been left behind by all of them. He felt that no one else had really loved his sister—neither his father, nor his mother, no one.

No one was sad at leaving her behind. Even though Didi was dead, the familiar haunts where they had played together, the paths, the bamboo forests, the mango groves—it was as though she had still been with him all this time. Didi's invisible loving touch had been with him in the broken-down house at Nishchindipur, in its every nook and cranny; but today, the separation between them was final.

Suddenly, Apu was filled with a strange feeling. It was neither sorrow, nor grief; exactly what it was he could not say. In a few seconds came a rush of memories . . . Aturi Witch . . . the ghat by the river . . . their house . . . the path by Chalta-tala . . . Ranudi . . . afternoons and evenings . . . days of laughter and play . . . Potu . . . his sister's face . . . his Didi's unfulfilled desires.

Didi was still looking and looking at them . . .

The next instant the unspoken feelings within him found expression in his tears and he wanted to affirm again and again, 'Didi, I have not left, I have not forgotten you, I did not want to leave you behind—they are taking me away.'

And truly he has not forgotten.

Apu grew up and came to know more intimately this planet girdled with blue foaming seas and vast open skies. But when—unconsciously shivering with the exhilaration of movement—he would gaze at the forever changing endearing forms of sky and sea from the deck of a seafaring ship, or, when a range of blue mountains thickly dotted with vineyards would gradually recede from his vision and merge with the distant horizon of the sea, and the dimly-seen coastline like the gift from a powerful artist-creator beckoned him like a mirage pulling in its tow his poetic self, he always remembered a monsoon night when amidst the deafening sounds of the unceasing rain in a dark room of a broken-down house a village girl, poor and fever struck— his Didi—saying to him, 'Apu, when I get better, will you show me a train?'

The distant signal of Majherpara station soon grew dim and finally disappeared from view.

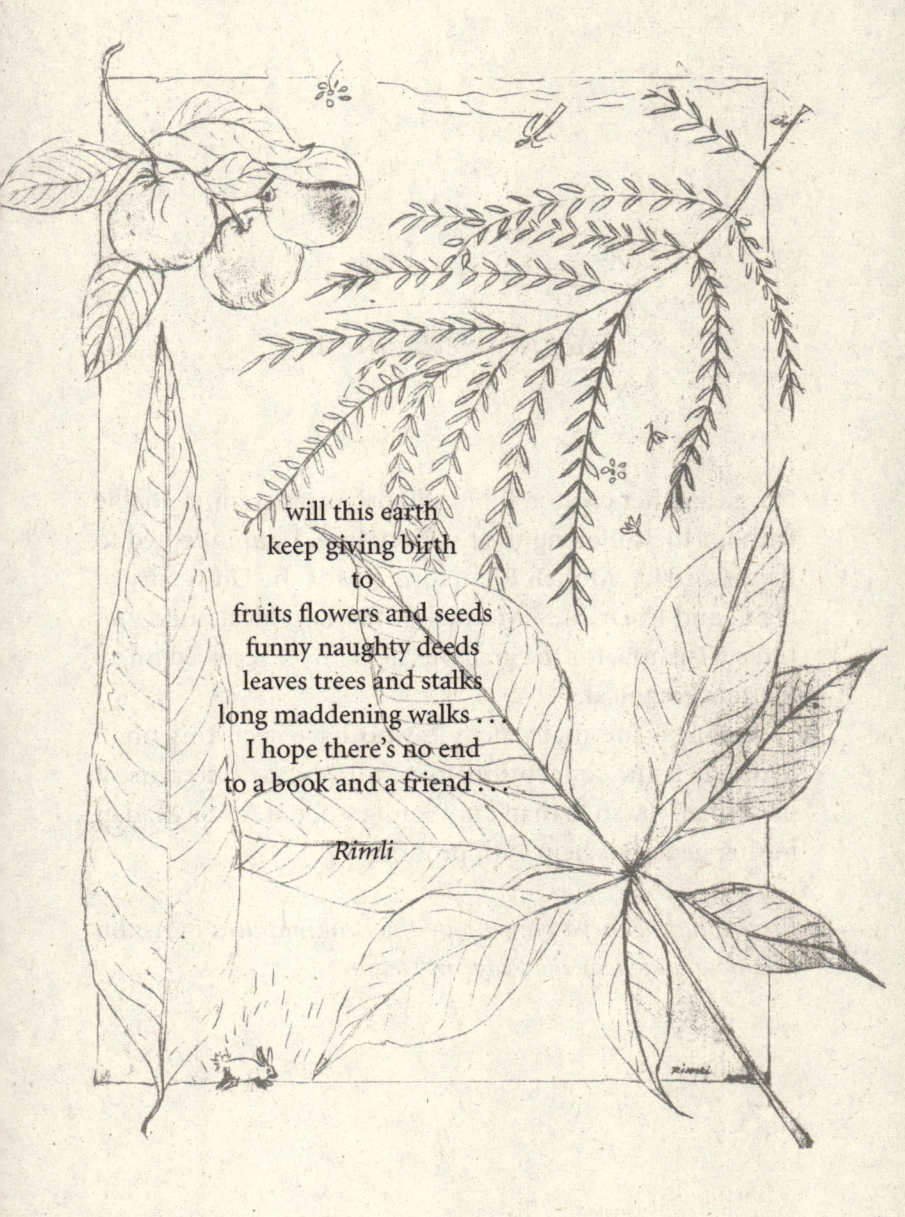

will this earth
keep giving birth
to
fruits flowers and seeds
funny naughty deeds
leaves trees and stalks
long maddening walks . . .
I hope there's no end
to a book and a friend . . .

Rimli

Acknowledgements

Durga and her creator, Bibhutibhushan, are unimaginable without their lifelong tryst with nature. I am indebted to Professor H.Y. Mohan Ram, formerly of the University of Delhi and to Dr M.S. Mondal of the Botanical Survey of India, Calcutta, for the gracious help I have received on all matters botanical.

Amongst the many people who have seen this book through from conception to a full-blooded creature I particularly wish to thank my young student Anuja Madan for her generous help with proofing.

Rimli Bhattacharya grew up by the Brahmaputra in Assam and now lives near the Ridge in Delhi.

The translator, whose name does not appear, and of the film maker
D.K. Gupta, the publisher, the Bangla Pather will be given
translation. The full title you get at the best possible on the
recurrent observation in might. Making a story life look
towards the precise and delicate balance that pervades the
Bibhutibhushan Bandopadhyay.

A note on the editions

*M*aking a Mango Whistle is translated from the Bangla *Aam
Anthir Bhenpu* considered the standard abridgement of
Bibhutibhushan Bandopadhyay's *Pather Panchali* (1929). This
special version for children was brought out during the author's
lifetime in 1944 by Signet Press, Calcutta. Roughly corresponding
to the second part of the three-part *Pather Panchali*, it is about
Apu and Durga's childhood, and has the same title as Part 2 of
the full-length novel. D.K. Gupta, the publisher, commissioned
Satyajit Ray, then a commercial artist, to illustrate *Aam Anthir
Bhenpu*. First published in 1944, the book has run into its thirty-
fourth edition in 2006.

Excepting for the first four chapters, this English translation
is based on the twenty-ninth edition of *Aam Anthir Bhenpu*
(Signet Press, 2003 [Chaitra BS 1410], 168 pp.). The first four
chapters, which end with the death of Old Indir, have been
recovered from the second edition of *Aam Anthir Bhenpu*
(Signet Press, 1944, 202 pp.). This edition has a total of

twenty chapters which are numbered and do not have titles. The first four chapter titles in this English version are the translator's. The titles, the contents and the frame of the remaining chapterization of *Making a Mango Whistle* follow those in the twenty-ninth edition of *Aam Anthir Bhenpu* which has nineteen chapters.

November 2006   Rimli Bhattacharya

PUFFIN CLASSICS

Making a Mango Whistle

With Puffin Classics, the story isn't over
when you reach the final page.
Want to discover more about the author
and his world?
Read on . . .

CONTENTS

NAME: Bibhutibhushan Bandopadhyay
BORN: 12 September 1894
MARRIED: Yes, he was married twice. He had one son, Taradas, from his second marriage.
DIED: 1 November 1950

What was he like?

Bibhutibhushan, like Sanyal babu in the story, loved travelling.

While working as a schoolteacher, he lived in various parts of Bengal, and from 1924 to 1930, he worked as an assistant manager of a vast estate of forestland in Bhagalpur district in Bihar. This was where he started writing his first novel, *Pather Panchali (Song of the Road)*. He travelled widely in many parts of the country, mainly in the north and the east. He would go on long treks, interacting with different kinds of people many of whom found their way into his writings.

Bibhutihushan had a wide-ranging curiousity about people and things, and he especially enjoyed reading about explorers and scientific discoveries. After his early childhood, he stayed in short stints in rural Bengal. He had tremendous compassion and empathy for village people and enjoyed being part of the extended network of village life.

What was his life like when he was young?

Bibhutibhushan's father, Mahananda Bandopadhyay, was a Sanskrit scholar. He was a pujari, or priest, and a kathakar, someone who composes and tells tales from the Puranas. The

young Bibhutibhushan often accompanied his father when he went on his rounds of storytelling and reciting poetry, and his father deeply influenced his creativity. Unfortunately, Mahananda died when Bibhutibhushan was very young. So he had to struggle against poverty from childhood and start working early in life, as a tutor and schoolteacher. Due to lack of money he had to drop out of college before he could complete his Master's degree, even though he was a talented student.

In 1917, while studying for his Bachelor's degree, he got married to fourteen-year-old Gauri Devi. But she died suddenly in a little over a year. Much later in life he married again.

What other books did he write?

Bibhutibhushan wrote novels, short stories, travelogues, and detailed diaries, all in Bengali. His literary career began in 1921 with the publication of the short story 'Upeksita' in the magazine *Prabasi*. He started writing his first novel *Pather Panchali* in 1925 when he was in Bhagalpur, and completed it in 1928. Its sequel *Aparajito* was published in 1931. His other important writings include *Meghamallar* (1931), *Mauriphul* (1932), *Aranyak* (1939), *Adarsh Hindu Hotel* (1940), *Smritir Rekha* (1941), *Devayan* (1944), *Hiramanik Jvale* (1946), *Utkarna* (1946), *He Aranya Katha Kao* (1948), *Ichhamati* (1950) and the posthumously published *Asani Sanket* (1959).

Bibhutibhushan also wrote for children, and the novel *Chander Pahar*, an adventure story set in Africa, is considered a classic.

How was Making a Mango Whistle *born?*

Bibhutibhushan's first novel, *Pather Panchali*, was recognized as a landmark in Bengali fiction soon after its publication. The book

was abridged for children, and was published as *Aam Anthir Bhepu* (*Making a Mango Whistle*), in 1944. *Making a Mango Whistle* primarily contains the stories of the children Apu and Durga, their days of growing up in Nishchindipur, along with vivid descriptions of village life and the countryside.

And in case you were wondering, the title of the book refers to the homemade whistle that is fashioned from a mango seed. Once the flesh has been eaten, the mango seed is left to dry. After a few days the outer skin is peeled off, and the softer seed inside is rubbed against a hard, abrasive surface. This seed can sprout again, and once the shoot is pulled out, it leaves a natural hole that is used to produce the sound.

The whistle is called *bhenpu* in Bangla, and *pipi* or *papiha* in Hindi.

KARNA'S STORY

Karna was the eldest son of Kunti, the wife of King Pandu of Hastinapur. Karna's father was Surya, the sun god. Kunti set Karna adrift in the river soon after he was born, as she was not married. A charioteer, a Suta by caste, rescued him and raised him as his own. As he grew to boyhood, Karna longed to acquire the skills of archery, the knowledge of which was reserved for the Kshatriya caste. When he approached Dronacharya, the teacher of the Pandava brothers, Karna was spurned as he belonged to a lower caste. Karna then approached Parasurama, the great sage, and pretending to be a Brahmin, tricked him into taking him on as a pupil. Parasurama taught Karna, but when he discovered that his student was really the son of a charioteer, he cursed him, saying that all the skills Karna had acquired would desert him at the time of his greatest need.

In the final battle of Kurukshetra, Karna fought along with the Kauravas against the Pandavas. When the duel between Karna and Arjuna began, Karna found that his trusted arrow, the Sarpaastra, could not kill Arjuna. A wheel from Karna's chariot got stuck in the mud, and while he was trying to free it, he was slain by Arjuna.

In the Mahabharata, Karna is symbolic of goodness and generosity.

SOME CHARACTERS IN THE MAHABHARATA

Bhima, son of Kunti and the wind god Vayu, his favourite weapon was the mace. He was the strongest of the five Pandava brothers.

Arjuna, son of Kunti and Indra, he wielded the Gandiva bow and was the best archer of the Pandavas. It was he who won Draupadi in an archery contest.

Bhishma, political advisor to King Pandu, he took the side of the Kauravas in the final battle. His father Shantanu had granted him the boon of *ichcha mrityu*, or the power to choose the time of his own death.

Duryodhana, son of Gandhari and Dhritarashtra, and the eldest of the Kauravas, he was jealous of Arjuna's skills and proclaimed Karna king of Anga. He was killed by Bhima in the battlefield of Kurukshetra.

A GLIMPSE OF LIFE IN A VILLAGE LIKE NISHCHINDIPUR...

Village life in Bengal in early twentieth century was strictly divided along caste lines. In fact, many localities, or paras, were named after the caste or occupation of the people living there, like Palit-para, Jele-para (fishermen's area), Bamun-para (Brahmins' area).

Many areas also got their names from a landmark tree or vegetation, like Chhatim-tala or Bakul-tala. The rivers and ponds where villagers bathed and washed clothes, as well as family temples and village shrines, were places to meet other people and gossip.

The old indigo bungalow in Nishchindipur was perhaps like many such 'kuthis' dotting Bengal and Bihar. Indigo dye was extracted from the indigo plant, which was grown on large plantations. The kuthis were a combination of factory, storage space and possibly living quarters for British plantation owners. Indigo kuthis were mostly built in the later part of the eighteenth century and some of them still survive.

Festivals and community celebrations were a constant, and the year was filled with exciting events like the Chariot and Charak festivals, as well as rituals dedicated to various gods and

goddesses, such as the one for Goddess Kuluichandi, when there was cooking outdoors.

However, the spectre of illness was never far away. Rural Bengal at this time was often in the grip of malaria outbreaks which killed people in the thousands.

The village school was usually a rough and ready place where the students got to learn the basics. The more gifted and ambitious students would then have to go to towns and cities for higher studies. Incidentally, in *Aparajito*, the sequel to *Pather Panchali*, Apu goes to Calcutta from Benares, to attend college. Later, he becomes a writer.

FAMILY RELATIONSHIPS IN BENGALI

Father	Baba
Mother	Ma
Daughter	Meye, referred to as Khuki affectionately
Son	Chheley, also referred to as Khoka
Elder sister	Didi, shortened to 'di' when added after a name, like Ranudi
Elder brother	Dada, shortened to 'da', like Satuda
Father's sister	Pishima
Bou	Daughter-in-law, but also used to address any young married woman

SOME THINGS TO THINK ABOUT

⋆ Have you read the stories of the Mahabharata? It is considered to be the world's longest epic. Which stories from Indian mythology did you enjoy reading, or watching on stage or TV?

⋆ At ten years of age, Durga is expected to share in the household chores. Which chores do you do in the house? Do you like doing them?

⋆ You must have noticed that there are no girls in Prasanna Guruji's school. Yet Durga, who is forever roaming outdoors, has a deep knowledge of plants. She introduces Apu to all the mysteries of nature. What would your ideal school be like?

⋆ Apu and Durga are fascinated by the railroad and the trains. Do you remember the first time you sat in a train? Did the railway station have anything in common with the station where Apu goes?

⋆ Have you ever explored old trunks in your house or read a book that belonged to your grandparents? What was it like to hold an object that belonged to someone many years ago?

⋆ Bini and her family lived separately from the other Brahmin families. Have you seen anyone being discriminated against because of his or her caste or religion? What were your thoughts when it happened?

⋆ The author had said once, that when he finished writing the first draft of his novel *Pather Panchali*, Durga did not appear in it. Can you imagine what this book would have been like without Durga?

⋆ Old Indir has a large stock of stories and rhymes which she teaches Durga. Have you ever met anyone like Old Indir? What is your favourite childhood rhyme?

GLOSSARY

Bengama and Bengami: a wise bird couple found in fairy tales

bhant: wild bush with fragrant flowers (also called ghentu)

bainchi: wild bushy shrub; the small violet-pink fruits have a sweet and sour taste

blue-throated bird: Indian roller bird

bon-chalta: wild tree with slightly bitter but edible fruit

chandrapuli: a fried savoury made with a sweet filling inside a layer of sweet potatoes and dipped in syrup

chhatim: also called saptaparna or the seven-leafed tree

Chariot festival: Rath-yatra, where models of a chariot are pulled in a large procession

Dashu Ray's Panchali: the full name of the author is Dasharathi Ray (1806-1857), a popular composer who had his own band of street poets; a panchali is a narrative poem which is sung. The title refers to his collection of verses on well-known stories from the Puranas and of local deities.

Dwaipayan Lake: in whose waters the wounded Duryodhana takes refuge after the battle of Kurukshetra. Betrayed by hunters, he is challenged to a mace combat and unfairly struck down by Bhima.

gajon: songs sung in honour of Shiva during the Charak season

Gandiva bow: one of the many supernatural gifts that Arjuna received from Agni, the god of fire, in exchange for letting him devour the Khandava Forest (and all its inhabitants) as his food. Krishna and Arjuna fought Indra, the god of rain, to keep their promise to Agni. The other gifts included a pair of quivers with

inexhaustible arrows and a divine chariot flying the Hanuman banner, along with superfast steeds.

gaub tree: tall and sturdy evergreen with sweet yellow edible fruit. The gum from the semi-ripe fruit is used in building houses, making boats, etc.

Gaurango: literally, one who has a fair or golden complexion; also another name for Chaitanya (1486-1533), from Bengal. Like him, his followers also celebrate devotional love, or prem bhakti, as a way of worship.

jatra: open-air drama with many songs and dances, performed by a troupe of travelling players. Boys enacted the female roles too. Traditional themes were from mythology (eg Krishna jatra), but there were also heroic pieces like the one that thrills Apu.

kulin Brahmin: considered superior to other Brahmins and could only intermarry. Therefore, kulin men usually had many wives who they visited rarely or occasionally.

luchi: fluffy rounds made of flour, deep fried in oil

makal: a climber with round tennis ball-size fruit; not edible but medicinal

Padma Purana: one of eighteen Puranas (or old narratives), relates the story of Chand Saudagar and his confrontation with the snake goddess Manasa; Shiva also has an important role. Long voyages and many interesting places are also described in this Purana.

pata: bright painting on the back of a shallow round earthen bowl, usually with a mythological theme, often used instead of a statue of the god or goddess; also a scroll painting

pathurkuchi: plant with thick leaves and big purple-red flowers; the paste of the leaves is used to heal cuts

rangchita: slipper plant or leadwort; used as fencing, also medicinal

Savitri-vrata: ritual of fasting and worship performed by a married woman for the well-being of her husband. It is named after Savitri who bravely faced Yama, the god of death, and brought back to life her dead husband Satyavan.

sheora: Siamese rough bush, the fruits are small and a brilliant yellow when ripe

shola: collected and made from the pith plant which grows in marshy waters. Artisans carve and mould the white and smooth sheets to create beautiful but fragile decorations, garlands, models and even deities

Shubhankari: treatise created by Brighuram Das (later known as Shubhankar) of Bankura, on mathematical calculations needed for everyday use; some formulae were in verse for easy memorization

Tarkalankar pandit: Sanskrit scholars or pandits were given titles based on their level of learning, like Tarkalankar or Tarkabagish. Apu's grandfather was called Pandit Ramchand Tarkalankar.

Vaishnav: follower of Vishnu, especially in his avatar as Krishna